Harriet B Audubon

Popular Fairy Tales in Words of One Syllable

Harriet B Audubon

Popular Fairy Tales in Words of One Syllable

ISBN/EAN: 9783337244682

Printed in Europe, USA, Canada, Australia, Japan

Cover: Foto ©Andreas Hilbeck / pixelio.de

More available books at **www.hansebooks.com**

ALADDIN : or, THE WONDERFUL LAMP.

POPULAR

FAIRY TALES

IN

Words of One Syllable.

BY

HARRIET B. AUDUBON.

With Eight Illustrations printed in oil colors.

NEW YORK:
LEAVITT & ALLEN BROS., PUBLISHERS.
1870.

TO

MY DEAR LITTLE NIECE,

LUCY,

THESE VOLUMES

ARE AFFECTIONATELY DEDICATED

BY

AUNT HATTIE.

PREFACE.

To those who have read *Robinson Crusoe* in words of one syllable, by Mary Godolphin, no further preface is necessary for any works of that kind. To those who have not read it, I would merely say, that although these have been called *Fairy Tales* in words of one syllable, it has been thought expedient to leave all the names unchanged, and also to retain certain other words, such as *fairy, princess, brother, sister, uncle,* which have no equivalent shorter than the words themselves, and without which it would be impossible to give to the stories the sense their author originally intended. My *young* readers, I know, will not criticise, and from those who are older, I hope for a just appreciation of the difficulties to be overcome, rather than a critical observation of the faults these volumes may contain.

H. B. A.

CONTENTS.

ALADDIN,

OR,

THE WONDERFUL LAMP.

In a town far to the East, there once dwelt a man whose name was Mustapha, who was so poor that he found it hard to earn bread to eat and to give to his wife and his son Aladdin. When the boy grew big, so that he could

work, his pa took him to his shop
and tried to teach him his trade,
but all he could do was in vain, for
Aladdin would not work. The
old man's grief for his bad ways
was so great that it made him ill,
and he soon died; and the ma,
when she found that her son
would not work, shut up the shop
and tried to earn bread for them
both by her own work. Aladdin
did all that was bad, till, one day,
as he was at play in the street, a
man who came that way, stood

still to look at him. This man was a wise man. He knew who Aladdin was, and how bad he was. He went up to him and said, "Child, was not your father's name Mustapha, and did he not make clothes?"

"Yes, sir," said Aladdin, "but he has been dead some time."

The wise man threw his arms round Aladdin's neck, and said, "I am your uncle; I have been twelve years from home, and now, when I have come back to see my brother, you tell me he is dead."

The wise man bade Aladdin kiss him, and gave him a ring, which he told the youth was worth much. He then led Aladdin a great way out of the town till they came to a spot with a hill on each side. He then set to work to pick up some dry sticks, and made a fire, and put on it some stuff that had a sweet smell, then he stood with his face to the sun and said some strange words, Al addin did not know what they meant. Then the earth shook, and the wind blew the sand from the spot, and the boy saw a stone with a ring in it, by which he could raise it up.

The wise man said, " Take hold of this ring, and lift up the stone, and you will find a thing of great worth, which shall be yours. Aladdin did as he was told, and took both his hands to raise the stone with great care. When he had done so he saw a cave.

The wise man bade him go down
and at the foot of the steps he would
find a door which led to three
great halls; at the end of these was
a yard, in which grew trees with
sweet fruit on them. "At the
end of that yard," said he, "you
will see a wall, and in it a niche,
and in the niche there is a lamp.
Take down the lamp, put out the
light, throw out the wick, pour
out the oil, and bring the lamp to
me." Aladdin sprang down the
steps of the cave, and found the

halls. He went through them, and then went on to the end of the yard and took down the lamp. As he went back he thought he would stop to look at the fine fruits which hung on the trees. Some bore fruit quite white, some red, some green, and some blue. Though he thought they were but glass, he was so struck with them that he took all he could hold, and then went back to the door of the cave. When he got there he said to the wise man:

"Uncle, give me your hand to help me up."

"Give me the lamp first," said the wise man.

"I can not, till I am up," said Aladdin.

The wise man would not help Aladdin to get out till he gave him the lamp; and Aladdin would not give it him till he was out of the cave. The wise man grew so wild with rage that he threw some stuff that had a bad smell on the fire, and said a few words; then the stone went back to its place, and thus Aladdin (who in vain cried out that he would give up the lamp) was shut up. The wise man, by his art, had found out that if he could get a lamp that was hid in some part of the world, it would make him as great as a prince. Then he found out that this lamp was in a cave in the land where Aladdin dwelt, in a vale, with a hill on each side of it. So he went to a town near to the cave where the

lamp was, and as he knew he
must take it from the hands of
some one else, he got Aladdin to
go with him.

When Aladdin had the lamp,
the wise man was in such haste to
get it, or was in such fear that the
boy would tell that he had it, that
he let it vex him, and so lost what
he came there to get.   He did not
think of the ring which Aladdin
had, and which he had told the
youth would keep him at all times
from harm, but went off in a huff,

with no ring and no lamp. When Aladdin found that he was shut up in this cave, he sat down on the steps and staid there two days; on the third day, he was so sad to think he could not get out of the cave, and so sick for want of food, that he put his hands on his head with a groan.

As he put up his hands he by chance gave a rub to his ring, and all at once a man of great height stood in front of him.

" What wouldst thou have with

me?" said this great, tall man; "I will mind thee as thy slave, whilst thou hast that ring on thy hand."

Aladdin said, "I know not who thou art; but take me from this place, if thou canst." Then the earth shook once more, and he was at the place where the wise man had built the fire. Aladdin ran home as fast as he could, and told his ma all he had seen and done. She was in a great rage at the vile man, and it made her sad to think that she had no food to give her son, who had had none for three days. Aladdin then made haste to show her the lamp, and said, "Ma, I will take this lamp and sell it, to buy us food, but I think if I were to clean it first, I could get more for it." So he sat down to wash it and rub it with sand. Then there came forth a great, tall man and said, "What wouldst thou have? I will mind thee as thy slave, and as the slave of all who may have the lamp which is now in thy hand."

Aladdin said, " Bring me food."
Then the tall man went off, but
soon came back with some nice
food on twelve plates made of
gold. He laid them down and
was no more seen. Aladdin and
his ma sat down and ate; they
had food to last till the next night,
when Aladdin took the plates and
sold them, and the price that was
paid for them bought them food
for years. One day Aladdin saw
a princess as she went to the baths.
He was so struck with her fair

face that he ran home to ask his ma to go to the Sultan and ask if he might make her his wife.

His ma thought he must be mad, and tried to make him give up his wish, but he said he could not live if he did not have the princess. He then brought his ma the fruit which he had got in the cave, and told her to take it as a gift to the Sultan, for it was fit for any king. He had found out that the fruits he thought were glass, were gems of great

worth.   So his ma went to where
the Sultan dwelt, and gave him the
gems in a vase.   He took the
gift, and when he had heard what
she had to ask, he said, "I can
not let my child be the wife of a
man till he sends me some great
gift; yet, if at the end of three
months from this day your son
will send me not one vase, but
four times ten of them, just like
this one, full of such gems, each one
borne by a black slave, and each of
them led by a white slave in fine

clothes, I will let him take my child for his wife. The Sultan did not wish his child to be the wife of one whom he did not know; but he thought Aladdin could not get the things he spoke of, so it would be the same as to say no, and yet would not be rude to the young man. Aladdin's ma went home and told him what he would have to do to make the Sultan grant his wish.

His joy knew no bounds when he found he should soon have the

princess.   As soon as his ma left
him, he took the lamp and gave it
a rub; then the same tall man
came to ask him what he would
have.   Aladdin told him what
the Sultan had said, and that the
things must be had at the right
time.   The tall man said it should
be done.   At the end of three
months the tall man brought the
black slaves, each one with a vase
full of gems, and with them were
the white slaves too.   Aladdin's
ma put on a fine dress and went

with them to where the Sultan
dwelt. When the Sultan saw
the long line of black and white
slaves, and that each of the black
ones had a vase full of rich and
rare gems, and that all their
clothes were like the clothes of
kings, he did not think he need
ask if in all things Aladdin was
fit to be the son of a king. The
sight of such great wealth, and
Aladdin's zeal to get the things
he had told him he must have,
made the Sultan sure that he was

fit to be his son, so he said to the
young man's ma, "Go, tell thy
son that I want to see him, and
that he may take my child to be
his wife." When Aladdin's ma
was gone, the Sultan got up from
his throne and told them to take
the gems to the room of his child.
The ma of Aladdin soon got back
to her son. "You are to have
what you wish," said she to him;
"the Sultan waits to see you and
make you his son." Aladdin, in
great joy at this news, went to

his room to rub the lamp. The tall man came. " I wish to bathe," said Aladdin, "then, give me a grand robe such as no king in all the world has yet worn." The tall man then took him to a bath where he felt some one rub and wash him in a bath that had a sweet smell, yet he saw no one. His skin grew clear and soft, he put on a rich robe, and the man then took him back to his room, where he did not fail to ask Aladdin what else he could do

for him. "Bring me a horse,"
said Aladdin, "and give me
slaves to go with me, and let each
one wear a rich robe. Give my
ma, too, six slaves to wait on her,
each one with a rich dress; but
more than all, bring me ten bags
with more bits of gold in them
than a man could count in a day.
The tall man went off and came
back with a horse, four times ten
slaves, ten bags, and six more
slaves, each one of whom had
a rich robe for Aladdin's ma.

Aladdin gave six of the bags to the slaves, that they might give the gold to the crowd as they went to the Sultan's home. He then sent one of the slaves to ask when he might go to the Sultan and fall at his feet. The slave brought him word that the Sultan would see him at once. When he came to the gate of the grand house where the Sultan dwelt, all the great men of the court went with him to the hall of state; there one of them gave him his hand to help

him off his horse, and led him to
the Sultan's throne.   The Sultan
did not know what to think when
he saw how rich Aladdin's dress
was, but he rose from his throne,
and gave him a kiss.   The next
thing he did was to wave his hand,
and the air was full of the sound of
lutes and harps and flutes and all
things that make sweet sounds.
He then led Aladdin to a large
room where food was laid for a
great feast.   Then the Sultan sent
for the chief man of law of the

place and told him to see that all
things were right to make the
princess the wife of Aladdin.
The Sultan then said to Aladdin,
" Do you wish my child to be your
wife this day ?" To which he said,
" Sir, I beg your leave to put it off
till I have built a house fit for the
princess, and I beg you too, to grant
me a spot of ground near your
own house, and I will take care to
have it built as fast as can be."
"Son," said the Sultan, "take what
ground you like." Then he once

more gave a kiss to Aladdin, who
took leave of him and went home.
He went to his room, took his
lamp, gave it a rub, and the tall
man came. "Build me a house,"
said Aladdin, "near the Sultan's,
fit for my spouse the princess; but
I will not have stone; let the walls
be made of gold and jet, laid in
rows, and in the cracks let there be
pearls and rich stones. The house
must have a large yard full of
sweet shrubs and plants that bear
nice fruits. But most of all, let

there be a great deal of gold coin. And there must be barns full of hay and corn, and in each barn twelve stalls, and in each stall a fine horse, and grooms to take care of them." By the dawn of the next day the tall man came once more to Aladdin, and said, "Sir, your house is built, come and see if it is what you wish." He had not time to say more than that he would go, when the tall man took him there. He found the house still more grand than he thought it

would be.   Then the tall man led
him to a small room which was full
of bags of gold up to the roof.
Then the tall man took Aladdin
home.   It was not yet the hour
when he might go through the
gates of the Sultan's house.   While
the Sultan was still in bed, some
of his men came to the gates, and
from there they saw Aladdin's
house ; they went straight to the
Sultan and told him of it.   " You
know," said the Sultan, " that it
is Aladdin's house, on the ground

which I gave him. When Aladdin had done with the tall man
he told his ma it was time for her
to go to the Sultan's house with
her slaves, and tell the Sultan she
came to go with the princess,
when the sun had set, to the house
of her son. Then Aladdin left
his old home, but he took care to
have with him his lamp, by the aid
of which he had grown so great.
At the house of the Sultan they
met Aladdin's ma with great joy,
and took her to the room of the

sweet princess.   The princess
came forth to meet her with much
love, and while they put on her
the gems which Aladdin had sent,
a grand feast was laid for them.
At night the princess took leave
of the Sultan and went to Aladdin's house.   His ma went with
her, and then came a long train of
slaves in rich robes.   In front
were bands that did not cease to
play gay tunes till they came to
Aladdin's house, and next came
the black slaves.   A long line of

the Sultan's young men held lights
on each side ; these, with the bright
lights of the Sultan's house, and
Aladdin's, made it like day. When
the princess came to the new house
Aladdin, full of joy, went with
haste to meet her. He took her
by the hand and led her to a room
where a grand feast was set out.
Each dish was of gold, and they
had in them nice food of all kinds.
The cups and plates were all of
gold, with such good work on them
that it was worth more than the

gold they were made of. Aladdin led the princess and his ma,
each to her place in this grand
room, and as soon as they sat
down there was a fine band to
play sweet tunes while they ate.
When the feast had come to an
end, Aladdin gave his hand to the
princess to dance with her, and
there were no more feasts that
night.   The next day Aladdin
got on a horse, and with a troop
of slaves with him, went to the
Sultan's house.   The Sultan met

him with great love, and gave him
a seat by his throne. Aladdin
did not stay in his own house and
the Sultan's, but rode through the
town and went to all the mosques.
He went, too, to see all the great
men of the court, and now, rich
and poor, all whom he knew,
grew fond of him. He might
have gone on thus a long time
had it not been for the wise man,
who, when he heard of Aladdin's good luck, said, " This boy
has found out the use of the

lamp, but I will not let him keep
it long. Next day he set out, and
soon came to the town in the
East where Aladdin dwelt. The
first thing he had to learn was
where Aladdin kept the lamp.
He soon found out by his art that
it was in Aladdin's house, and to
know this gave him great joy.
He found out, too, that Aladdin
had gone off to hunt, and would not
come home for eight days. The
wise man then went to a man who
made lamps, and bought twelve,

which he put in a pack on his back. He went thus to Aladdin's house, and when he came near it he cried, " Who will change old lamps for new ones ?" This strange cry brought a crowd of men and boys, who thought he must be mad to give new lamps for old ones; yet still he did not cease to cry, " Who will change old· lamps for new ones ?" This he said so oft near Aladdin's house, that his wife sent one of her slaves to know what the man

cried. " Ma'am," said the slave,
" it makes me laugh to see a fool
with a pack full of new lamps on
his back, which he wants to
change for old ones." Then a
girl who stood by, said, " I
know not if the princess has seen
it, but there is an old lamp up
stairs; if the princess likes she may
try if this man will give a new
one for it." This was Aladdin's
lamp, which he had left up stairs
when he went off to hunt, but
the princess had not seen it, nor

had those who were with her.
Aladdin, as a rule, took the lamp
with him when he went to hunt;
but this time he left it at home.
The princess, who knew not how
much the lamp was worth, bade
one of the slaves take it and
change it. The slave went and
gave a loud call to the wise man,
held up the old lamp, and said,
"Will you give me a new one for
this? The wise man knew this
was the lamp he came to get, so
he took it from the slave, and

bade him take that which he
thought the best ; the slave chose
one and took it to the princess.
As soon as the wise man got out
of the gate of the town, he stood
still, and spent the rest of the day,
till it was night, in a wood near
by, when he took the lamp and
gave it a rub. The tall man
came. " I bid thee take me,"
said the wise man, " with the
house thou has built for Aladdin,
and all who live in it, to a place
a great way off. Then the tall

man took him and the house of
Aladdin, and all in it, to a place
a great way off, which the wise
man told him of. Next day,
when the Sultan went, as was his
wont, to his door to look at Aladdin's house, he saw but a space
of ground, with no house on it.
This made him so wild with rage
that he knew not what to do. He
cried, "Where is that man, that
I may have his head cut off;
send out a troop of men to bring
him to me in chains." The troop

went as they were bid, and, twelve miles from the town, they met Aladdin on his way home ; they told him that the Sultan had sent them to fetch him home. Aladdin had not the least fear, and went on his way, but when they were half a league from the town the chief of the troop said, " Prince Aladdin, the Sultan bade me bring you to him in chains." So they put chains on both his arms, and in this way he had to walk to the town. When the troop came near the town, all who saw Aladdin thus led in chains had no doubt that his head would be cut off, and as they all were fond of him, they took swords, and spears, and all kinds of arms, and those who had none took up stones and went with the troop and in this way they came to the Sultan's house.

They took Aladdin to the Sultan, who, as soon as he saw him, said that his head should be cut off. So the man who was to

cut his head off, took off the chains
and made him kneel down; then he
drew his sword and stood still till
the Sultan should give the sign
for him to cut off Aladdin's head.
Just then a vast crowd of men
from the town burst through the
gate that led to the Sultan's
house.   When the Sultan saw the
men he told them that Aladdin
should not be slain. When
Aladdin found that he was free, he
went to the Sultan and said to
him, " I beg you to let me know

my crime." "Thy crime!" said the Sultan. "Come with me." The Sultan then took him to his room. When he came to the door he said to him, "You ought to know where your house stood : look and tell me where it is now." "I beg you," said Aladdin, "to give me twelve days to try to find out." "I give you twelve days," said the Sultan. For three days Aladdin did naught but walk from place to place till he could walk no more. At the close of the third day he came to the bank of a stream, and as he had lost all hope, he thought he would jump in and put an end to his life.   He thought it right to pray first, and went to the stream to wash his hands and face, for it was the law of the land that a man should wash his face and hands first, and then pray.   The bank of the stream was steep and moist, and as he trod on it he slid down by a small rock.   As he fell down the bank a stone hurt his hand and gave his ring a hard rub.   At once the same tall man came forth, whom he had seen in the cave. Aladdin said, "I bid thee take me to the place where my house stands, and set me down where the princess can see me if she looks out." The tall man took him to a large plain, on which his house stood, and set him down on a bank close to the house where the princess could see him when she rose, and there left him. The next day one of the girls saw Aladdin, and told the princess, who could not think that she spoke the truth, yet she ran to look out, and saw Aladdin. She said to him, " I will send a slave to let you through one of the gates." When Aladdin got in he went to the princess's room and gave her a kiss, and then he said to her, " Do you know where an old lamp is, which I left at home when I went to hunt?" The princess told him that she had been such a goose as to change it for a new one, and that the next day she found she was in a land she did not know.

The man who gave a new lamp for
the old one took her there by his
art. "Princess," said Aladdin, "I
know now who this man is; he is
the worst of all men; but this is
not the time or place to tell you
all the wrong he has done. Can
you tell me what he has done with
the lamp, and where he has put it?"
"He takes it at all times with him;
this I know, for once he took it
out of his robe and let me see it."
"Princess," said Aladdin, "tell me,
I pray you, how this bad man

treats you." "Since I have been here," said the princess, "he has come once a day to see me, and I am sure that he would come more than once, if he saw that it gave me joy to see him. He tries in vain to make me love him more than you, and wants to make me his wife. He tells me not to hope to see you, that you are dead, that the Sultan had your head cut off. He says too that you are a wretch ; that you owe your good luck to him, and all such things. He finds that I have no love for him, and he sees my grief and tears, and he goes off sad. I have no doubt he means to wait some time, to see if I cease to grieve for you; and if I do not, he will make me his wife by force. But now you have come, my fears are all gone." "I am glad," said Aladdin, "that my wife feels no fear, and I think I know how to save you from that bad man. I shall come back at noon, and will then tell you what I mean to do, and what you must do to help me. But I must first tell you that I shall change my dress, and I beg of you to tell your slaves not to let me wait long at the gate but to let me in at the first knock. The princess said she would take care that all this should be done. When Aladdin went out of the house, he met a man in the road, and said to him, "My good man, will you change clothes with me?" the man said he would. So they went to the back of a hedge and the man took

Aladdin's clothes, and Aladdin took his. Then Aladdin came to the town and went to that part of it where the shops were. There he found a man who sold drugs, and he bought half a drachm of a drug that he told him the name of. Aladdin went back to the house, and when he saw the princess he told her to ask the wise man to sup with her. "Then," said he, "put this drug in one of the cups of wine, charge the slave to bring that cup to you, and then change cups with him; as soon as he has drank it, he will fall dead. When it was time to sup, the wise man came, and they sat down side by side. The princess gave him part of all the good things there were, and said to him, "If you please we will change cups, and I will drink your health and you may drink mine." He took her cup with joy. The princess put the cup to her lips, while the wise man drank his to the last drop, and fell back dead. Then Aladdin came in and said,

"Princess, I must beg you to leave me for a short time." When the princess was gone, Aladdin shut the door, went to the dead man, took the lamp out of his vest, and gave it a rub. The slave of the lamp came. "I bid thee," said Aladdin, "take this house to where it stood at first." The house then went back to where it had been, yet none who were in it felt it move. Aladdin went to the princess's room and gave her a kiss, and said, "I can tell you, princess,

that your heart and mine will soon
be full of joy." Next day Aladdin
rose with the dawn, and put on one
of his best robes. When it was
just light, he went to the door, gave
a look out, and saw the Sultan.
They met at the foot of the great
stairs of Aladdin's house. The
old Sultan could not speak for
some time, so great was his joy that
he had found his child once more.
She soon came to him; he gave her
a kiss and made her tell him all
that had come to pass. Aladdin

told his slaves to throw the wise man's corpse on a rock, as the prey of birds. Thus Aladdin was safe from his arts. The Sultan died at a good old age, and as he left no sons the princess was to be queen; but as she was Aladdin's wife, the great men of the state said that he should rule. There was to be a great feast when Aladdin put on his crown. In all the East, none had seen so great a feast as this was to be. At length the day came. There was such a crowd it took them some hours to get to the great mosque. Aladdin sat on a throne, and they had just put a crown of gold on his head, when . . . . he woke, and found that it was all a dream: he had slept with his head on his father's shop-board.

BEAUTY AND THE BEAST.

THERE was once a rich man, who had three boys and three

girls. As he was a man of good
sense, he took great pains to have
them taught all that it was right
for them to know, and did his
best to get all the wise men of the
land to teach them. The two
first girls were by no means plain,
but the third was still less so; in
truth she had so sweet a face,
and so fine a form, that she got
the name of the Little Beauty, and
as she was still the same when
she grew up, she kept that name.
Her sisters did not like their

friends to love her more then them,
but they all did so, and this made
them cease to care for her.   It
gave all who knew them, joy to
look at this girl's sweet face ; and
her kind heart, too, made them
love her.   The two big girls were
proud of their wealth, and spoke
with pride to those who they
thought were not so rich as they
were.   They were full of airs,
and would not go to see the girls
who had less wealth than they
had.   They went each day to

balls, plays and walks, where they met gay crowds, and made game of their sister, who read, or sat at her work, and did what was of use. As it was well known that these young girls would be rich at their pa's death, some of the men who had large stores in the town, thought they would like to get them for wives, but the two big girls said that, for their part they would be the wives of none but dukes or earls at least. There were not a few who thought they would have cause to be proud, if they could have had Beauty for a wife, but to all who told her so, she said with a sweet smile, that she gave them thanks, but she did not wish to leave her father for some years, as she thought she was too young to be a wife.

It came to pass that, by some sad chance, the rich man all at once lost his wealth, and had then naught but a small house and farm far from the town. So he said to his girls, while the tears ran down his cheeks all the time, " My girls, we must now go and live in our small house, and try to earn our bread by our work, for there is no way but that for us to live." The two big girls said that, for their part, they did not know how to work, and would not leave town, for there were scores of men who would be glad to make them their wives, though they had lost their wealth. But this they found was not so, for when the men heard what had come to pass, they said, " The girls were so proud and cross that we did not want them, we did but ask them for the sake of their wealth ; we are glad to see their pride brought down ; let them put on their airs to their cows and their sheep." But all were sad to see poor Beauty lose her wealth, she was so sweet and good to all who knew her, and more than one man would have been glad to make her his wife, though she had not a cent. But

Beauty would not; she said she could not leave her poor father, in his grief, and would go and help him in his work far from the town. At first, (when no one saw her,) Beauty cried, when she thought of all she would have to bear, but in a short time she said, " It will do me no good if I cry my eyes out, so I will try not to be sad, though I have lost my wealth. When they had gone to their small house, to make it their home, her father and his three sons

spent their days in the fields, at the
plough, and when the sun set, they
came home and did what work
they could in the yard near the
house, till it grew too dark for them
to see. Beauty, too, did her part,
for she got up at the dawn of day,
and made the fires,and swept the
house. It was she who put the
meat to boil, and the bread to
bake, and did not cease to watch
them while they were on the fire,
lest they should burn. At first
she found all this hard, but soon

she got to like it, and did not think it hard at all; and she grew quite strong and well, which she had not at all times been. When she had done her work she would read, or play on her harp, or sing while she spun. But her two sisters were at a loss what to do to pass the time. They took their first meal in bed, and did not rise till ten. Then they took a walk, but they did not care to walk far; they would soon sit down in the shade of a tree and grieve for the loss of their coach and fine clothes, and would say, "What a goose our young sister is, to like so well our low way of life!" But their father did not think at all as they did. The sweet ways of his dear girl were his best joy, for her sisters left her to do the whole work of the house, and made game of her all the time. When they had spent a year and some months in this way, the man got a note which told him that one of his rich ships, which he thought was lost, had just come to land. This news made the too big girls half wild with joy, for they thought they should now leave the small house, and have rich and gay clothes once more. When they found that their father must go a great way off, to the ship, the two big girls ran to him to beg that he would not fail to bring them back some new gowns, caps, rings, and all sorts of fine things. But Beauty did not ask him to bring her fine things, for she thought that all the ship was worth would not buy all the fine things her sisters had told him to bring. "Beauty," said her father, "can it be that you have no wish for fine things? What can I bring you, my child?" "Since you are so kind as to think of me, dear father," she said, " I should be glad if you would bring me a rose, for we have none in our yard." Now, in truth, Beauty did not wish for a rose; she had no wish at all; but she said this that she might not vex her sisters, for if she had said that she had no wish, they would have thought she said so, that their father might praise her more than them. He took his leave of them and set out on his way; but when he got to the ship, some men went to law with him for the things that were on board of it. He had to wait a long time, and then set out to go back to his small house, as poor as he had left it. When he was but twelve miles from home, as he rode, he thought what joy it would be to see his girls once more;

but his way lay through a thick
wood, and he was lost.   Then a
storm came on, the rain and hail
fell thick and fast, and the wind was
so high as to throw him twice from
his horse.   Night came on, and he
thought to be sure he should die
of cold and want of food, or be torn
to bits by the wolves that he heard
howl all round him.   All at once
he cast his eyes to where there
was a long row of trees, and he saw
a light at the end of them, but it
was a long way off.   He went up

to it as fast as he could, and found
that it came from a fine house with
lamps in all parts of it. He went
on with still more speed, and soon
got to the gate, which he went
through, and strange to say, he saw
no man, nor beast, nor fowl, in the
yard. His horse had come in
with him, and as it found a barn,
the door of which was not shut, it
went in at once, and here the poor
beast, who was in great want of
food, ate a good meal of oats and
hay. The man then tied him up

and went to the house. He went in, but still did not see a thing that had life. He went on, and came to a large hall where he found a good fire and some nice meat and bread; and one plate and knife and fork. As he was wet to the skin with the hail and rain he went up to the fire to get dry. "I hope," said he, "the man who owns this house, or the men who wait on him, will not find fault with me, for to be sure I shall soon see them now." He stood still a good while, but

no one came; at last he saw that
in one hour it would be twelve,
and as he was quite faint for want
of food, he took a fowl, which he
made but two bites of; then he took
a glass or two of wine; yet all the
time he shook with fear. He sat
till the clock struck twelve, but
saw no one. He now grew bold,
and thought he would look round
and see what was to be seen,
so he went to a door at the end of
the hall, gave one more look round,
saw no one, and made up his mind

to walk through the door. It led to a grand room, in which there was a fine bed, and as he was in great need of rest, he shut the door, took off his clothes and lay down. It was ten the next morn when he woke. Up he sprang with a bound, but he did not know what to think, when he saw a fine new suit of clothes laid out for him in place of his own, which had had so much harm done to them by the rain, that they were not fit for him to wear. " To be sure," said he, "this is the house of some good fairy, who has seen my bad luck, and is kind to me." He gave a look out of doors, and he saw large groves, in which there were fine, gay plants. He went back to the hall where he had had so good a meal the last night, and found some tea and toast and all sorts of good things laid out for him. "In truth, my good Fairy," said he in quite a loud tone, "I thank you for your kind care of me." He then made a good meal, took his hat, and left the hall, to go to the barn to see his horse; but, as he went by a bush on which was a pure white rose, he thought of what Beauty had said she would like him to bring back to her, so he took out his knife and cut the rose from its stem, that he might take it home with him. Just then he heard a loud noise, and saw such a fierce beast come up to him, that he felt as if he should drop with fear. "Vile man," said the beast, in

a voice full of rage, "did I save
your life for this? I let you come in
my house and get warm, and eat
and sleep, and to pay me for that
you steal from me my white rose,
which was more to me than all
else that is mine; but you shall
pay for your fault with your life;
you shall die in less than half an
hour." The man fell on his knees
to the beast, and held up his hands
to him and said, "My lord, I beg
you not to kill me; I did not think
it would vex you, if I took a rose

for one of my girls, for when I left home I said I would get her gowns, or rings, or books, if she would but tell me what; but all she would ask for was a rose." " I am not a lord, but a beast," said the beast, " I do not like false names. I like men to say what they mean ; so do not think that you can coax me by such ways. You tell me that you have girls. Now I will let you live if one of them will come and die in your place.   Go, but first give me your

word that you will come back in
three months, if none of your girls
will come in your place." The
good man did not mean to let one
of his girls die in his place, but he
knew that if the beast thought he
would do what he told him, he
should see them once more, which
would make his heart glad. So he
gave his word to the beast, and
the beast then told him he might
set off as soon as he thought best.
"But," said the beast, "I do not
wish you to go back till you have

got what you like, to take with you. Go to the room you slept in; you will find a chest there ; fill it with just what you like best, and I will have it sent to your own house for you." When the beast had said this he went off, and the good man thought, " If I must die, it will be joy to me to leave my girls some wealth." He went back to the room he had slept in, and found a great deal of gold coin. He put the gold in the chest till it was full up to the brim, then he shut it up tight, got on his horse, and left the house, as full of grief now as he had been full of joy when he found it.

The man did not pull the rein, but let his horse choose his own path through the wood, and in a hour or so they got home. His girls ran to meet him as he got off his horse, but the man could not kiss them with joy : his eyes were full of tears, as he put his arms round them. He held in his hand the white rose he had cut off the bush, he gave it to Beauty, and said, "Take this rose, Beauty, but you do not know how dear it has cost your poor father," and then he told them all he had seen and heard in the house of the beast. The two big girls now shed tears, and laid the blame on Beauty, who they said would be the cause of her father's death. " See," said they, " what comes from the pride of this girl ; why did she not ask for fine things as we did ? but, to be sure, Miss must not be like the rest of us, and though she will be the cause of her father's death, yet she does not shed a tear!" "It would be of no use ," said Beauty, "to weep for the death of my father, for he shall not die now. As the beast will take one of his girls in his stead, I will put my life in his hands ; and I shall be glad that I can at the same time prove my love for, and give up my life for the best of fathers." "No, sister," said the three sons, "you shall not die ; we will go in search of this beast, and he shall die, or kill us all three." "Do not hope to kill him," said their father; "he is too strong to let you do such a thing. I am glad to see that Beauty has the same kind heart she has had since she was a babe; but I will not let her lose her life. I am old, and can not live long, so I shall give up but a few years of my life, and it would not grieve me at all, were it not for my boys and girls." "No, father," cried Beauty, "you shall not go to the beast's house and leave me at home, for you can not keep me here when you go; though young, I am not too fond of life, and it would please me more to have the beast eat me up, than to die of the grief your loss would cause me." The man tried in vain to make Beauty think as he did, for she would go, which, in truth, made her two sisters glad; for they still had the same old fault to find with her, which was, that all who knew them would love her more than

they could love them.   Her father
was so full of grief at the thought
that he should lose his child, that
he did not think of the chest full
of gold till night, when he found
it by the side of his bed.   He did
not tell his big girls that he had a
chest full of gold, for he knew it
would at once make them want
to go back to town; but he told
Beauty of it, and let her see it,
and she then said that while he
was gone, two rich men had been
to their house to see them, and

they fell in love with her two sisters
and would like to make them
their wives. She then told her
father that it would please her if he
would let these rich men take
them for their wives soon, for she
was so good and kind that she
felt great love for them, though
they had shown none for her, for
she was too good a girl to let her
thoughts dwell on the wrongs
they had done her. When the
three months were past, Beauty
and her pa set out to go to the

house of the beast. The two
sisters could not cry; they were
too glad ; so they took a kind of
root that makes the eyes smart, to
rub their eyes with, to make their
father think that they shed tears ;
but both he and his sons cried hard ;
so all cried but Beauty; she did not,
for she thought that would but
make things worse. They got to
the beast's house in a few hours,
and the horse, though no one told
him to do so, went straight to the
same barn where he found such

good cheer when he was there the last time. Beauty and her father went to the large hall, where they found all sorts of good things for them to eat, and two plates, one for each of them. Beauty's father did not eat much, but she, to hide her grief, sat down and put some food on her father's plate ; then she tried to eat, and thought all the time that to be sure the beast had a mind to make her fat, so that he would find her good to eat, as he had got such good cheer for her. When they had got done their meal, they heard a great noise, and the good old man bade his poor child good by, for he knew that it was the beast he heard. When Beauty first saw his huge form, she shook with fright, but she tried to hide her fear as much as she could. The first thing the beast did was to ask her if she had come quite of her own free will, and though she was now half dead with fear, she said, "Yes." "You are a good girl, and I thank you,"

said he. He then said to her pa,
"Good man, you may leave this
place at dawn of day, and take
care that you do not come back.
Good night, Beauty." "Good
night beast," said she, and then the
beast went out of the room. "Ah,
my dear child," said Beauty's pa, as
he gave her a kiss, "I am half
dead with the thought that I must
leave you with this vile beast; do
you go back, and let me stay in
your place." "No," said Beauty,
that shall not be; you must go

home at dawn of day." They
then said good night and went to
bed. They both of them thought
they could not sleep a wink ; but
as soon as they had lain down,
they went to sleep and did not
wake till near dawn. Beauty
had a sweet dream, which was
that some one, with a pure white
dress on, came to her and said,
" It gives me great joy Beauty,
to see what a kind heart you
have. It was your wish to give
your life to save that of your father ;

that was kind and right, and you shall live to be glad that you have done so." As soon as Beauty woke, she told her father this dream, but though it gave him some hope, he shed tears as he took leave of his dear child. When he was out of sight, Beauty sat down in the large hall and cried as if her heart would break ; yet she had a strong, brave heart, so she soon made up her mind not to make her sad case still worse by grief, which she knew could be of no use to her, but to wait as well as she could till night, when she thought the beast would not fail to come and eat her up. In the mean time, as no one came to her, she went up stairs and down stairs, and took a full view of all the house. So grand a house she had not seen in all her life. But who can tell how queer she felt, when she came to a door on which she read the words, *Beauty's Room.* She went in, in haste, and it made her eyes and her heart glad to see such a room. What gave her more joy than all, was that one side of the room was full of shelves on which were books. She saw, too, a harp, to which she could sing the sweet songs she had sung in her own home. " The Beast takes care I shall not be at a loss how to spend my time," said she. She then thought that the beast would not have put all these things here for her, if she had but one day to live, and it gave her hope that all would not turn out so bad as her fears. She went to the shelves where the books were, and saw these lines on the gilt back of one of the books :

Fair girl, dry up your tears,
You have no cause for fears ;
Say what you wish to see,
And it shall come to thee.

"Ah!" said she, with a sigh, "what I most wish is to see my poor father, and to know where he is, and if he has got back to our house."

She said this in so low a tone that
no one could hear her; but just
then, by chance she cast her eyes
on a glass that stood near her, and
in the glass she saw her home
and her pa, who, on his grey nag
rode up to the door of the house
in great grief.   Her sisters came
out to meet him; but for all they
tried to look sad, one could see,
with ease, that in their hearts they
were full of joy.   In a short time
the things that she saw went out
of the glass; but Beauty thought

that the beast was a good, kind beast, and that she had no need to fear him. When it came to be noon, she found rich food set out for her, and she heard sweet sounds, like harps and the songs of boys and girls, all the time she ate, and yet she saw no one. But, at night, when it was tea time, and she sat down in her seat, to eat the nice food she found laid out for her, she heard the noise of the beast, and it made her shake with fear. "Beauty," said he, as he came in, "will you give me leave to see you sup?" "That is as you please," said she, in great fear. "Not at all," said the beast; "no one but you shall have the right to say what shall be done in this place. If you do not like to see me here, you have but to say so and I will leave you to take your tea in peace." Beauty thought of her room, and the things he had put there to please her, and she told him to stay if he would like to do so. "Tell me, Beauty," he said then,

do you not think I am a fright?"
"Why yes," said she, "for I can
not say what is not true, but
then I think you are good and
kind." "You are right," said the
beast; I am a fright, and then I am
dull too.   I know full well that I am
but a beast." "I do not think you
can be dull," said Beauty, "if you
know this."   "Pray do not let me
keep you from your tea," said he,
"and be sure you ask for all you
want, for all you see is yours, and
it will give me much grief if you

are not glad and gay." "How kind you are!" said Beauty. "I must needs own that I think well of your kind heart, and then I do not think what a fright you are." "Yes, yes, I hope I have a good heart," said he, "but still I am a beast." "There are men who are worse beasts than you are," said Beauty, "and you please me more in that form, though it is the form of a beast, than those who have bad hearts, with the form of a man." "If I had the least sense," said the beast, " I would thank you for what you have said, but I am so dull that I do not know how to say what would please you." Beauty took her tea with a gay heart, and felt as if she should soon lose all her dread of the beast, but she thought she should sink with fear when, all at once, he said to her, " Beauty, will you be my wife?" For a short time she could not speak a word, for she thought he would fly in a great rage if she said no. At length she said, " No, beast." The beast did not speak, but he gave a deep sigh, as he left the room.

When Beauty found that he had gone, she felt sad as she thought of him. "Dear me," said she, "what a sad thing it is that he should be such a fright, since he has such a good heart!" Beauty dwelt three months in this house, and was, most of the time, quite gay. The beast came to see her at night. He said it gave him joy to see her, and talk with her, while

she took her tea, and though
what he said was not as wise as
what some men might have said,
yet, as she saw in him, each day,
some new mark of his good heart,
she did not dread the hour when
he came to see her; far from that,
she would look at her watch three
or four times to see if it was near
nine; for that was the time he
came to pay his call. There was
but one thing that gave her pain;
this was, that each night, as the
beast went out of the room, he

made it a rule to ask her if she would be his wife, and he grew more and more sad each time that she said no. At last, one night, she said to him, "You vex me much, beast, when you ask me to be your wife, for it gives me pain to say no to you. I wish I could like you so well as to be your wife ; but I must tell you the truth, which is, that I do not think such a thing can be. I shall be your friend all my life, so try not to wish for more than that." " I must needs do so, then," said the beast, "for I know full well what a fright I am, but I love you more than I love my life. Yet I think I have good luck when I find you are so kind as to stay with me. Now give me your word, Beauty, that you will not leave me." Beauty was quite sad when he said this, for that same day she had seen in her glass that her father was sick with grief for her sake, and that the thought that he should see her no more, made him so ill that they thought

he would die. "I will, with all
my heart, give you my word that
I will not stay far from you," said
she, "but I long so much to see
my father, that if you do not give
me leave to go to him, I shall die
with grief." "I would as lief die
as see you fret, Beauty," said the
beast. "I will send you to your
father's house ; you shall stay there,
and your poor beast shall die of
grief." "No," said Beauty, and
she cried while she spoke, "I love
you too well to be the cause of

your death.   I give you my word
that I will come back in a week.
You have shown me in my glass,
that both my sisters are now wives,
and live in their own homes, and
my brothers are gone to the wars,
so that my poor father has no one to
stay with him.   Let me stay one
week with him."   "You shall be
with him at dawn of day," said
the beast, " but mind that you keep
your word to me.   When you
wish to come back all you will have
to do will be to put your ring

on a chair when you go to bed. Good by, Beauty." The beast gave a sigh as he said these words, and Beauty went to bed with a sad heart to see him in such grief. When she woke the next morn, she found that she was in the house of her father. She rang a bell that was at the side of her bed, and a maid came in ; but as soon as she saw Beauty, she gave a loud shriek ; when Beauty's father heard the shriek, he ran up stairs, and when he saw his dear girl, he felt

as if he should die of joy. He ran
to the side of the bed and gave
her a kiss with a glad heart.
When it was time for Beauty to
get up, all at once the thought
came to her, that she had brought
no clothes with her, to put on; but
the maid told her that she had just
found, in the next room, a large
chest full of clothes, with fringe of
gold round the neck and sleeves,
and on the skirt, and with the
gold, there were pearls of great size.
Beauty, in her own mind, gave

the beast her thanks for this kind act, and chose a gown that was not so gay as the rest. She then told the maid to put the rest in some safe place with a great deal of care, for she meant to give them to her sisters ; but as soon as she had said these words, the chest was gone out of sight, in less time than in would take you to count ten. Her father then said that he thought the beast meant that she should keep them all, and that no one else should wear them ; and as soon as he had said this, they saw the chest stand in the place where it had stood when Beauty first spoke of it. When Beauty had her dress on, a maid brought word to her, that her sisters had come, with the men whose wives they were, to pay her a call. These men did not love their wives much, and did not live in peace with them at all times. One of these men had a fine face and form, but was so proud of this that he thought of it from morn to night, and did not care at all how his wife might look. The sister who was next in age to Beauty, was the wife of a man who knew a great deal, but he made no use of what he knew but to tease and vex all who came near him, and his wife more than them all.

The two sisters felt as if they should burst with spite, when Beauty came down stairs to see them. They could not bear to see her look so fair and so well. All the kind things she said to

them were of no use, and their
rage knew no bounds when she
told them what nice things she
had in the house of the beast.
These bad girls left her in the
house, and went off to the yard,
where they cried to think of her
good luck. " Why should we be
worse off than this bad girl?" said
they. " Her face is not half so
fair as ours." " Sister," said the
worst of the two, " I have just
thought of a plan to get rid of
her ; let us try to keep her here

more than the week that the beast
gave her leave to stay, and then
he will be in such a rage that no
doubt he will eat her up as soon
as he sees her." " That is well
thought of," said her sister, " but
to do this we must make her
think that we are fond of her."
So they made up their minds to
be kind to her, and went to join
her in the house, where they gave
her so much false love that her
heart was won and she cried for
joy. When the week was at an

end, the two sisters spoke so much
of their grief at the thought that
she must leave them, that she
said she would stay a week more.
But all that time there were sad
thoughts in Beauty's heart, that
she could not drive out, for she
thought how sad her poor beast
would be, when he found that she
did not go back to him, and now
her whole heart was full of love for
him and the wish to see him grew
more and more strong. The
tenth night that she was in her

father's house, she had a dream. She thought she was in the yard at the back of the. house of the beast, and that he lay more than half dead, on a grass plat, and with his last breath put her in mind of what she had said to him. He told her that she had not kept her word, and that that was the cause of his death. Beauty woke in a great fright, and tears fell from her eyes. "Am I not a bad girl," said she, " to treat so ill a beast who has been so kind to me? Why will I not be his wife? I am sure I should have more joy and peace with him, than my sisters have with the men whose wives they are. He shall no more be sad to find that I do not go back, for if he should die I should feel all the rest of my life that it was my fault." She then rose, put her ring on a chair, then went back to bed and soon went to sleep. The next morn, how great was her joy to find that she was in the house of the beast. She rose and put on her best dress, that she might please him more. " Oh that the night would come !" said she. As the hours went by, one by one, the day was to her like ten days. At last the clock struck nine, but the beast did not come. Beauty then felt sure she had been the cause of his death in truth. She ran from room to room, till she had been in all the rooms of the house, but she could not find him. An hour went by, and still her search was not at an end. All at once she thought of her dream, and ran straight to the grass plat and there she found the poor beast. At the first look she gave, she thought all sense had left him. He was, as far as she could see, quite dead. She threw her arms round him, She did not think then what a fright he was, and as she found that his heart still beat, she ran to fill a jug at a spring in the yard, and knelt down by his side, to bathe his face. The beast then tried to look up at her, and said, "You did not keep your word, Beauty. I felt so sad to think that I had lost you that I could not eat, and now you see how near death I am; but I can die in peace, it is such joy to see you once more." "No, dear beast," said Beauty, "you shall not die, you shall live; I will be your wife, and no man shall have the right to take me from you, as long as we both live. Oh, I thought I was but your friend, but the pain I now feel, shows me that I could not live if I did not see you." As soon as Beauty had said these words, the house of the beast was full of light, and the sweet sound of harps, and fire-works, and all things that tell of great joy, were seen and heard. But Beauty saw and heard none of these things. All her heart was with her dear beast, by whose side she knelt, and whom she did not cease to watch with great love. But now, as her eyes were still cast down, she saw at her feet, not her poor beast, but a prince in a rich dress, with as fine a face and form as you could wish to see. This prince gave her his thanks that she had been so kind to him. She did not know what to think, but all she could do was to ask this young prince where the beast had gone. "You see him at your feet, Beauty," said the prince, "for I am he; a bad fairy said that I should keep the form of a beast, till some fair young girl should say that she would be my wife; and this fairy told me, on pain of death, not to show that I could speak or act with sense. No one but you, dear Beauty, would judge of me by my heart, and to pay you for that I will give you my hand and my crown, though I know that that is much less than what I owe you." Beauty, with a heart full of joy and love, gave the prince her hand to help him to rise, and then they went to the house, and who can tell what joy

she felt to find there her father and
sisters, who had been brought there
by the fairy Beauty had seen in
her dream the first night she slept
in the beast's house. " Beauty,"
said the fairy, "you will, all your
life, be glad of the choice you
have made. You chose a good
heart, and thought more of that
than of sense or a fine face, and
you shall find them all three in
the same man. You will soon be
a great queen ; I hope, when you
wear a crown, you will not cease

to be as good and true as you are now. As for you," said the fairy to Beauty's two sisters, " I have long known the bad thoughts of your hearts, and the wrongs you have done. You shall change to two white posts, but in that form you shall still keep your mind, and see and hear all that goes on. Your place shall be at the front gate of your sister's house, and I can not wish you more pain than it will give you to see her joy. You will not change back to your own forms till your faults have quite left you, and to tell you the truth, I much fear you will be posts till the end of the world." Then the fairy with a stroke of her wand took all who were there to the land of the young prince, where all who had known him in times past, came forth to meet him in great joy. He took Beauty for his wife, and spent a long life with her. They were all the time full of joy and peace, for they did right in their thoughts and words and acts as they had done all their lives.

THE CHLDREN IN THE WOOD.

THERE once dwelt, long since; when you were not yet born, in a land a great way off, a man and his wife; the man had a brave, kind heart, and all who knew him

felt great love for him, and his wife
was just such a wife as a good man
like him ought to have. They
tried at all times to do kind acts to
those who came to see them, or
whose homes were near theirs, or
who did work for them, and it
was these kind acts and kind
words that they gave to all, that
won for them so much love. The
man and his wife dwelt in one
house for years, in great peace and
joy, for the man felt great love for
his wife, and she felt the same for

him. They had a boy and a girl, who both were still quite young, for the one who was born first, who was a boy, was not quite three years old, and the one who was born last, who was a girl, was not quite two years old. The boy was a good deal like his father, and the girl was a good deal like her mother. By and by the man fell sick, and day by day he grew worse. His wife, as I have just said, gave to him her whole heart, and it was such grief to her to see how ill he was that she fell ill too. The drugs that they took to cure them, and all the nice things that their friends brought, were of no use, for they grew worse and worse; and they saw that death would soon take them from their two dear babes, and that they would have to leave them in the world with no father and no mother to take care of them. They bore this sad thought as well as they could, and they had hopes that when they were dead, their babes would find some kind friend who would take them and bring them up as their own. The man spoke of this to his wife, but he did not know what he ought to do with them, and his wife was as much in doubt as he was; but at last he said that he would send for his brother, and place the dear babes in his care. As soon as the man's brother heard this news, he made all the haste he could, to go to the place where the father and mother lay sick, and in a short time he stood by the side of their bed. "Ah! brother," said the man, as he lay on the bed of death, "you see how short a time I can hope to live; yet death and pain can not give me half so much grief as I feel at the thought of what these dear babes will do with no father or mother to take care of them. Brother, brother," the man went on to say, and he put out his hand as well as he could to point to the babes, "they will have no one but you to be kind to them, no one but you to see that they have clothes and food, and to teach them to be good and wise."

" Dear, dear brother," said his wife, who was as near death as he was, "you must be father and mother and uncle too, to these dear lambs. First let Will be taught to read, and then he should be told how good his father was. And dear, dear Jane, oh brother, it wrings my heart to talk of her. Think of the kind love she will be in need of, and take her up and set her on your knee, brother, and she and Will will pay you for all your care of them, with the love of their whole hearts." The uncle then said, "Oh, how it grieves my heart to see you, my dear brother and sister, in this sad state; but keep a brave heart; there may still be hope that you will get well; yet if it should come to pass that we must lose you, I will do all you wish for your dear babes. In me they shall find a father, a mother and an uncle. Will shall be taught to read, and from time to time I will talk to him of his father and tell him how good he was, that he may turn out as good when he grows up to be a man. I will take great care of Jane, and will take her up in my lap, and show her all the love I can. But, dear brother, you have not said a word of the great wealth that will be left here when you are dead. I am sure you know my heart too well to think that I speak of this for my own sake ; it is for the good of your dear babes that I speak, so that I can make use of all your gold for their sake." "I pray, brother," said the man, who had not now half an hour to live, "do not say such a thing ; it grieves my heart to hear you, for how could you, who will be their father and mother and uncle too, once think to do them wrong? Here, here, brother, is my will. You will see that I have done the best I could for my babes." When the man had said these words, he put his cold lips to the soft warm lips of his babes; his wife did the same, and in a short time they both died. The uncle shed a few tears at this sad sight, and then went to get the will, in which he found that his brother had left the boy, Will, the sum of three hundred pounds a year, when he should be of age, and to Jane, the girl, the sum of five hundred pounds in gold to be paid her the day a man took her to be his wife. But if the boy and girl should chance to die while they were still young, then all that their pa had left to them, was to be their uncle's. The will of the dead man next said that he and his dear wife should be laid side by side in the same grave. The boy and girl now went home to the house of their uncle, who for some time did just as their father and mother had told him, as they lay on the bed of death. Each day they saw signs of his great love and they thought he must care more for them than for all else in the world. But when some months had gone by he thought no more how their father and mother gave them to his care, and how he gave his word that he would be their father and mother and uncle all in one. This change did not take place all at once, but day by day his heart grew more and more cold to the babes whom he had said he would take care of. When some more time had gone by it came to the uncle's heart to wish that the boy and girl would

die, for then he should have all
their wealth to keep for his own ;
and when he had once thought
that, he went on till it put all else
out of his head. At last, one day,
he said in his own mind, "It would
not be a hard thing for me to kill
them, so that no one should know
that I had done so, and then all that
their father left would be my own
at once. When the bad uncle had
once brought his mind to kill the
poor babes, who could not keep
him from it, it did not take him

long to find a way to bring it to
pass.   He got two strong and bad
men, who, in a dark, thick wood
some way off, had slain some of
those who went through the wood,
that they might get from them
their gold.   The uncle now spoke
to these two bad men, and they
told him that if he would give
them a great sum, they would do
the worst deed that man could do;
and so the uncle laid his plans to
help them as much as he could.
He told a false tale to his wife of

what good it would do to the boy
and girl to make them learn more
than they did, and how he had a
friend in a large town a great way
off, who would take care of them.
He then said to the poor things,
who were too young to think that
he would harm them, "Should
not you like, my sweet ones, to go
to a great town, where you, Will,
can buy a fine horse made of wood
to ride on all the day long, and a
whip to make him go fast, and a
fine sword to wear by your side?

And you, Jane, shall have new frocks, and dolls, and new toys, all the time, to play with, and a nice coach with gold on it shall be got to take you there." "Oh yes, I will go, uncle," said Will. "Oh, yes, I will go, uncle," said Jane, and the uncle, with a heart as hard as a stone, soon put their things in a trunk and in a few days he told them it was time to start. The poor things were put in a fine coach, and with them were the two bad men who would soon put an end to their sweet talk, and change their smiles to tears. One of them drove the coach, and one sat in it on a seat, with Will at his right hand, and Jane at his left. When they came to the dark, thick wood, the two bad men took them out of the coach, and told them that now they might walk for a short time and pick up nuts and play, and while the babes got out of the coach to play and skip like young lambs the bad men with their backs to them laid their plans for what they had to do. "In good truth," said the one who had sat with a child on each side all the way to the wood, "now I have seen the sweet babes, and heard them talk, I have no heart to do so bad a deed. Let us drop the sharp knife in the stream and send the babes back to their uncle." "But in truth I will not," said the man who drove the coach; what is their sweet talk to us?" "Think of your own babes at home," said the first. "I do think of them, and I

think that I shall not get the gold
to take back to them if I let these
babes live as you would have me
do."

At last the two bad men fell in
such a great rage, as they spoke
of the poor babes, that they had a
fight, and the one who would have
been glad to spare the lives of the
boy and girl, took out the great
knife he had brought to kill them,
and cut to the heart the man who
would have put an end to their
lives, so that he fell down dead at

his feet. The one who had slain him was quite at a loss what to do with the babes, for he now felt that he must run off as fast as he could for fear that some one would find him in the wood. At last he thought all he could do was to leave them in the wood, and hope that some kind man might pass that way and find them there, and take them to his own home, or back to their uncle. "Come here, my sweet babes," said he, "you must take hold of my hands and go a short way with me." The poor babes took each a hand and went on, but the tears burst from their eyes, and their limbs shook with fear all the while, for they had seen the two men fight, and did not know what would come to pass next. Thus he led them two or three miles on in the wood, and then told them to wait there till he came back from the next town, where he would go and get them some food. Will took his sister Jane by the hand, and they went in great fear up and down in the wood. "Will the strange man come soon with some cakes, Will?" said Jane. "By and by, dear Jane," said Will. Jane did not speak for some time ; then she said, " I wish I had some cakes, Will." Then they gave a good look round on all sides through the wood as far as their eyes could see, and it would have made a heart as hard as a stone, feel sad to see how sad their looks were, and how, when they heard the noise of the wind in the trees, they thought it might be some one come to help them. When they found that their hopes were in vain they tried to eat wild grapes, but they soon ate all that they could reach. Night came on, and Will, who had tried all he could to help his sister, who was not so old as he was, now felt the need of some one to help him; so when Jane said once more, "Oh Will, I do so want some food, I—I—I must cry, I can not help it." Will cried too, and down they lay on the cold earth, and Will put his arm round Jane's neck and Jane put her head on his arm; there they lay sick for want of food, and there they died. Thus these two sweet babes, who in all their lives had done no harm, met with a sad death, and as no one knew that they were dead, so there was no one to dig a grave and put them in it. In the mean time their uncle thought they been slain, as he had told the two bad men to kill them, so he told all the folks who tried to find out from him where they were, a false tale. He said that they had died in the great town, of the small pox, and he then took all their wealth for his own, and spent it as if it had been his by good right. But all this did him no good, for soon his wife died; the loss of his wife made him sad, and then, too, in the night, as he lay in bed and tried to sleep, he thought he saw the poor babes with blood on their clothes, so his wealth gave him no joy, and as he was too full of grief to make plans to keep it, or make it more, he lost it day by day, and soon came to be a poor man. Then, too, his two sons had gone on board of a ship to try to get rich far from home, and to see the world ; but they both were lost at sea, and he grew quite sad, and his life gave him no more joy. When things had gone on in this way for some years, the bad man who had gone with the babes to the wood and would not kill them there, tried to rob some one in that same wood. They gave chase to him, and he was laid hold of, and put in a cell; in a few weeks he was tried, and when the judge found that what they said of him was true, he said he should be hung for the crime. As soon as he found what his death must be, he sent for the man who kept his cell and told him all the bad deeds he had done in his whole life. Thus he made known the death of the two babes, and, at the same time, told what part of the wood he had left them to starve in. The news of this soon came to the ears of the uncle. At that time his heart was sad for all the ills that had come to him, and he could not bear the load of shame that he knew must now fall on him, in the sight of all the world. So he lay down on his bed, and died that same day. As soon as the tale of the death of the two babes was made known to the

CHILDREN IN THE WOOD.

world, some men were sent to search the wood for them. Their search was in vain for a long time, but at last the sweet babes were found side by side. Will's arm was round the neck of Jane, his face close to hers, and part of his frock lay on top of hers. There were leaves on them that quite hid them from view, and which, in all that time, had not grown dry; and on a bush, near this cold grave, there sat a robin red breast who took his place there to watch the grave and chirp, so that there are some who still think it was this kind bird that brought the leaves and laid them on the sweet babes.

WHITTINGTON AND HIS CAT.

In the reign of the great King Edward the Third, there was a boy whose name was Dick Whittington, whose father and mother died when he was a small child, too young to know them ; so that when they were dead he could not think of them, but was left a poor, young boy, all in rags, to run round in a small place far from all the great towns. As poor Dick was too young to work, he was at times in great want of food ; he had but a poor meal at noon, and there were some days when he had not a bite till then ; for those who dwelt in the small town were all poor, and could not spare him much more than a few beans, and now and then a hard crust. For all this Dick Whittington was quite a sharp boy, and took great pains to hear all that was said in the town. On the first day of the week, he was sure to get near the men who had farms, as they stood still to talk in the church yard, when the priest had not yet come. And once a week you might see Dick lean on the sign post of the chief ale house of the town, where the folks would go in to get a drink as they came from the next town.

And when the door of the shop where the men went to shave was not shut, Dick would hear all the news that the men who met there had to tell. In this way Dick heard some strange things of the great town of London; for the poor folks, who did not know much at that time, thought that all the men in London were lords and dukes, and that all the girls got to be the wives of those great folks, and they thought that all the streets had gold in them in, place of stones.

One day, a large cart, drawn by eight mules, with bells at their heads, drove through the town as Dick stood by the sign post. He thought that this cart must be on its way to the fine town of London; so he made up his mind to ask the man who drove, to let him walk with him by the side of the cart. When the man heard that poor Dick had no father or mother, and saw by his rags that he could not be worse off than he was, he told him he might go if he would.

So they set off side by side. I have not heard how it was that Dick got meat and drink on the road, nor how he could walk so far, for it was a long way; nor what he did at night, for a place to lie down and sleep in. It may be that some kind folks in the towns that he went through, when they saw how small he was, and that he was all in rags, gave him some food, and it may be that the man who drove the cart, let him get in it at night and take a nap.

These things may or may not be
so, but Dick got safe to London,
and was in such haste to see the
fine streets that had gold in them
in place of stones, that I fear he
did not stay to thank the kind
man who had let him come with
him, but ran off as fast as his legs
could take him, through the streets,
for he thought all the time that he
would soon come to those that
were full of gold; for Dick had
seen a gold piece three times, in
his own town, and knew how

much change it brought; so he
thought he had but to take up a
small piece of the stone and
would then have all he could wish
for. Poor Dick ran till he could
run no more, and thought no more
of his friend who had brought
him to town ; but at last, as he
found that it grew dark, and that
each way he went, he saw naught
but dirt in place of gold, he sat
down in a dark nook, and cried
till he went to sleep. Poor Dick
was all night in the streets, and the

next day, as he was in great want of food, he got up and went from place to place, to beg all who went by to give him a few pence, but no one staid to speak to him, and but two or three gave him some pence ; so that the poor boy was soon quite weak and faint for want of food.   At last a man with a kind face came by and saw him look as if he would be glad of a piece of bread to eat. " why don't you go to work, my lad ? " said he to Dick.   " That I would," said Dick, "if I knew how to get some work." "If you will work," said the man, "come with me;" and as he said this, he took him to a hay field, where Dick was glad to work with all his might and live a gay life till the hay was all made. Then he soon found that he was once more in great want of food, and he lay down at the door of Mr. Fitzwarren, a rich man who kept a large store and sent out ships to sea. Here he was soon seen by the cook maid, who was a cross thing: she said to poor Dick, "What do you want here, you rogue? the town is full of boys who beg. If you do not walk off at once, we will see how you will like me to pour some soap suds on you, that are so hot that they will make you jump." Just at this time Mr. Fitzwarren came home to dine, and when he saw a boy, all rags and dirt, at his door, he said to him, "Why do you lie there, my lad? you are not too small to work, I fear you have not the wish to do so." "In truth, sir," said Dick to him, "that is not the case, for I would work with all my heart, but I know no one, and I think I am sick for want of food." "Poor boy!" said Mr. Fitz-warren, "get up and let us see what ails you." Dick now tried to rise, but was too weak to stand, for he had had no food for three days, and could not run round and beg pence of folks in the streets. So the kind man told them to take him in the house and give him some good food, and he said that he should be kept there, to do what work he could for the cook.   Dick would have been full of joy in this good man's house, had it not been for the cross cook, who did naught but find fault and scold him from morn till night.   At last some one told Miss Alice, Mr. Fitzwarren's child, how cross the cook was to him; she said to the cross thing, "Do you not think it a shame to be so cross to a poor boy who has no father or mother?"

and she told her, too, that she should lose her place if she were not more kind to him. But though the cook was so cross, the man who stood at the back of the coach when Mr. Fitzwarren drove out, was not so at all; he had been in the house some years, and was quite an old man. He had once a son of his own, who died when he was Dick's age, so he grew fond of the poor boy, and at times gave him some pence to buy cake or a top, for tops did not cost so much

then as they do now. This man
was fond of a book, and at night,
when the men and maids had done
their work, he would read to them.
It gave Dick great joy to hear
this good man read, and it made
him wish to learn to read too ; so
the next time his kind old friend
gave him some pence, he bought
a book with it, and with his help
he soon knew how to read. Just
at this time Miss Alice went out
one day for a walk, and as the
man whose place it was to wait

on her at such times, was out of
the way, and as Dick had a suit
of good clothes that Mr. Fitzwarren gave him to go to church
in, he was told to put them on,
and walk near her. As they
went on, Miss Alice saw a poor
thing, with one child in her arms
and one at her back. She took
out her purse and gave her some
pence ; but when she meant to
put her purse by, she let it fall on
the ground and went on. It was
well that Dick was near and saw

what she had done.   He took up
the purse and gave it to her.
Then, one day, as Miss Alice sat
in her room to play with a pet
bird, all at once it flew off to the
branch of a high tree, where none
of the men would dare to go and
get it.   As soon as Dick heard
of this, he took off his coat, and
ran up the tree like a mouse.   It
was quite a hard task to catch the
bird, for Poll thought it was fine
fun to hop from branch to branch,
but he caught her and brought

WHITTINGTON AND HIS CAT.

her down safe to Miss Alice, who
gave him her thanks, and was still
more kind to him than she had
been. The cross cook was now
not quite so cross, but there was
one more hard thing that Dick
had to bear. His bed, which was
of straw, stood in a small room at
the top of the house, where there
were holes made by the rats in
the floor and the walls. At night
they ran on his face, and made
such a noise that he would wake
from his sleep. One day a man

who came to see Mr. Fitzwarren, said that he would like some
one to clean his shoes ; Dick took
great pains to make them shine,
and the man gave him two pence.
With these he thought he would
buy a cat, so the next day, as he
saw a girl with a cat in her arms,
he went up to her to ask her if
she would let him have it for two
pence. The girl said she would,
with all her heart, for her ma had
more cats than she could keep.
She told him, too, that this one

knew well how to catch mice.
Dick hid his cat in his room, and
took good care to share his food
with her, and in a short time there
were no more rats and mice there,
and he slept as well as he could
wish. Mr. Fitzwarren had a
ship that was soon to sail, and as
he thought it right that all his
men and maids should have some
chance to grow rich as well as he
had, he sent for them to his room to
ask them what they would send out.
They all had goods of some kind

that they were glad to send out,
that is to say, all but poor Dick ; he
had no pence and no goods to
send, so he did not go to Mr. Fitzwarren's room with the rest; but
Miss Alice knew why he did not
come, and sent for him ; she then
said she would lay down some
pence for him, from her own
purse, but her pa told her this
would not do, for Dick must not
send what was not his own.
When poor Dick heard this, he
said all he had was a cat which he

had bought for two pence. "Fetch your cat, then, my good boy," said Mr. Fitzwarren, "and let her go." Dick went up stairs and brought down poor puss, and gave her to the man who had charge of the ship, with tears in his eyes, for he said now he should not sleep all night for the rats and mice. It made them all laugh to think what an odd thing it was that Dick sent, but Miss Alice felt sad to think how poor Dick was, and she gave him some pence to buy a new cat.

This and some more kind acts
that Miss Alice did, made the
cross cook hate poor Dick, and
she beat him more than she had
done, and made game of him, for
no cause but that he had sent his
cat to sea. Then she would ask
him if he thought his cat would
sell for as much as would buy a
stick to beat him with. At last
poor Dick could bear this no more,
and he thought he would run off
from his place; so he took the few
things he had, and set out at dawn

on All Saint's day. He went as far as Holloway, and there sat down on a stone (which to this day bears the name of Whittington's stone) to think what road he should take next. As he sat still to think, the bells of Bow Church (which at that time had but six bells) rang out their chimes, and he thought they said to him:

Turn again, Whittington,
Lord Mayor of London.

" Lord Mayor of London !" said

he. " Why, to be sure, I would
put up with all things now, to be
Lord Mayor of London, and ride
in a fine coach, when I grow to
be a man ; well, I will go back,
and not mind all the cuffs and
harsh words of the old cook, if I
am to be Lord Mayor of London
at last."   Dick went back, and by
good luck, got to the house in
good time, and was hard at work
when the old cook came down
stairs.   The ship with the cat on
board was a long time at sea, and

the winds drove it, at last, to a
wild coast, where the men from
the land where Dick was, had
not been till then. Those who
live there are Moors. The folks
of that land came in great crowds
to see the ship and the men on it ;
they did not know what to make
of them at first, for they were
white, and the Moors were black ;
they were kind to them, and when
they knew them well, were glad to
buy the fine things on board of
the ship. When the man who

had charge of the ship, saw this, he sent some of the best things he had to the King of the land, who thought them so fine that he sent for him and his chief mate to come to his house. Here they sat down on rich cloths, on the floor, which is the way they all do in that land. The King and Queen sat at one end of the room, and rich food was brought in for them all to eat; but as soon as the food was there, great troops of rats and mice ran in, and ate from all the plates, and threw the sauce and bits of the meat to all parts of the room. The mate thought this quite strange, and said to the King's slaves; "Do you not find these rats and mice quite in the way?" "Oh, yes," they said, "and the King would give half his wealth to get rid of them, for they waste his food, as you see, and they run round so in his room at night, that some one has to watch him all the time he sleeps for fear of them. The mate felt as though he should jump for joy when he heard this. He thought of poor Dick's cat, and told the King he had a beast on board his ship that would kill all the rats and mice. The King was still more glad than the mate. " Bring this beast to me," said he, "and if it can do what you say, I will give you your ship full of gold for her. The mate, to make quite sure of his good luck, said that she knew so well how to catch rats and mice, that he did not like to part with her, but that,

to please the King, he would fetch
her. "Run, run," said the Queen,
"for I long to see her, since you
say she will do us so much good."
Off went the mate to the ship,
while they got some more food.
He took puss in his arms, and
came back to the house of the
King, and found the room full of
rats and mice. When the cat saw
them, she did not wait to be told,
but gave a jump from the mate's
arms, and in a short time laid a
great part of the rats and mice

dead at her feet. The rest of them, in a fright, ran off to their holes. The King and Queen were full of joy to get so well rid of such plagues, for in their lives, they had not had a meal in peace by day, nor a good sleep at night. They said they would like the beast that had done them so much good, to be brought for them to look at. On this the mate said," Puss, puss," and the cat ran up to him, and sprang on his knee. . He then held her out to the Queen, who gave a start back, and did not dare to touch a beast that could kill such a crowd of rats and mice ; but when she saw how good the cat was, and how glad it made her to have the mate stroke her, she grew so brave as touch her too. At last the Queen took her on her lap, and there puss went to sleep. When the King had seen what puss could do, he bought all the goods that were in the ship, and then gave him a great deal of gold, which was worth still more, for the cat. The man who had charge of the ship then took leave of the King and Queen, and the great men of their court, and with all his ship's crew set sail with a fair wind for the land of his birth, and got there in a short space of time. One day, when Mr. Fitzwarren had just come to his room where he wrote, and sat down at the desk, some one came tap, tap, tap, at the door. " Who is there?" said Mr. Fitzwarren. "A friend," said some one, as he

came in at the door ; when who
should it be, but the man who had
charge of the ship, and the mate,
just come back from the wild
coast where the wind drove them;
next to them came some men
who had in their arms great lumps
of gold, that had been paid by the
King for the things on board the
ship. They then told how they
had sold the cat, and gave Mr.
Fitzwarren the rich gift that the
King had sent to Dick for her; then
that good man said to his men :

Go fetch him, we will tell him of the same ;
Pray call him Mr. Whittington by name.

Mr. Fitzwarren now let them see what a true, good man he was, for when some of his clerks said so much gold was too much for such a boy as Dick, he said, " God grant that I may not keep the worth of two pence from him ; it is all his own, and he shall have it, and no one else. He then sent for Dick, who at that time had to scour the cook's pans, and was by no means clean, and did not like to go and be seen in that plight, so he sent word he could not go for fear the great nails in his shoes would spoil the smooth floor. But Mr. Fitz-warren made him come in, and had a chair set for him, so that poor Dick thought they meant to make game of him as the men and maids did down stairs; and he said, "I beg you, sir, not to play tricks with a poor boy, but

let him go back to his work."
"In truth, Mr. Whittington," said
Mr. Fitzwarren, "we all mean
just what we say, and I am
glad of the news these men have
brought you, for your cat has been
sold to the King of a wild coast
where they had none, and he has
sent you, for her, more gold than
I have in the whole world, and I
give you joy with all my heart.
Mr. Fitzwarren then told the
men to show Dick the great
lumps of gold they had brought

with them, and said, "Mr. Whittington must now put it in some
safe place. "Poor Dick did not
know what to do for joy. The
first thing he did was to beg
Mr. Fitzwarren to take what
part of it he chose, since it was he
who told Dick to send his cat.
"No, no," said Mr. Fitzwarren,
"this is all your own, and I have
no doubt you will use it well."
Dick next said to Mr. Fitzwarren's
wife, and then to Miss Alice,
"Will you not let me give you

part of my gold?" But they would not, and at the same time told him that they were glad his cat had sold so well. But the poor boy had too kind a heart to keep it all, so he gave a good deal to the man who had charge of the ship, the mate, and all the crew, and then to his good friend who stood at the back of the coach when Mr. Fitzwarren drove out, and to the rest of the men; he was so good that he did not leave out the cross old cook. Then Mr.

Fitzwarren told him he had best send for some men who sold coats, and those who sold boots, and hats, and put on a dress such as a rich young man ought to wear, and told him he should be glad to have him live in his house, till he could find one to suit him. When Dick had had the good taste to wash his face and curl his hair, and had on a new hat and a nice suit of clothes, his face was quite as good as those of the young men who came to see Mr. Fitzwarren and

his wife and child, so that Miss
Alice, who had been so kind to
him, now thought him quite fit to
be in love with her, and the more
so, no doubt, as Dick now all the
time tried to please her, and made
her gifts that cost great sums.
Mr. Fitzwarren soon saw how
much they were both in love, and
said he would make them man
and wife, which gave them great
joy. They did not take long to
fix the day when they would be
made one, and the Lord Mayor

and a great crowd of rich men went
to the church with them. When
they left the church they had a
fine feast. It is said that Dick
and his wife had a gay life and
were full of joy. They had some
boys and girls, who were all good
and gave them no grief. He was
more than once Lord Mayor of
London; the last time he was so,
King Henry the Fifth went to
dine with him, when he got back
from the great fight of Agincourt.
While he was there, he said of

Whittington. "Few Kings have such a subject." When Whittington was told this, he said, "Few subjects have such a King." For some brave deed of his, the King made him a knight. Sir Dick Whittington fed the poor, built a church, and a good school, and paid for those who were too poor to pay. Near the school he built a house for the sick. Some men who knew how to carve stones and wood, made Sir Dick Whittington in stone, with his cat in

his arms.   It was to be seen till
the year 1780, on the old arch
that stood in Newgate Street.

END OF FIRST SERIES.

CINDERELLA ;

OR,

THE LITTLE GLASS SLIPPER.

THERE was once a rich man who
lost his wife, and as he had been
fond of her, her death gave him
great pain. He was so sad when
he had no wife that he thought he
would take a new one, and then
he might be as full of joy as he

had once been. But the wife he chose was both proud and cross to all who knew her; no one could please her, and to those who were with her, she was as rude as she could be. She had two girls by the first man whose wife she had been, and she brought them up to be proud and to do no work; in their minds and in their rude ways they were just like their mother; they did not love their books and would not learn to work; in short no one could like them.

The man on his side too had a child, a girl who, with her sweet smile and kind heart, was just like her own mother, for whose death he had felt so much grief. He was in hopes that his new bride would take care of his dear girl, as her own mother would have done if she had not died. But as soon as she came to her new home, one could see what a bad heart she had. She could not bear the dear child, for her sweet ways made those of her own girls seem much

worse. So she made her live
down stairs with the cook, and if,
by chance, she came to the room
where she was, she did not cease
to scold her till she was out of
sight. She made her work with
the maids, and wash the plates, and
cups, and knives, and forks, and
rub the chairs, and sweep and
dust the grand rooms where the
bride and her two girls slept.
The walls were gay and bright,
and in each room was a glass so
long that it could well nigh reach

from the top of the room to the floor, and so broad as to touch both sides of the room ; while the poor child who kept the rooms neat had to sleep in a room at the top of the house, on a poor straw bed with coarse sheets, and too few clothes to keep her warm. The poor child had to bear all this. She did not dare to tell her father, whom she thought would but scold her, for she saw that his wife made him do all that she thought would be good for her and her two girls. When she had done her work, she used to sit down by the fire, and her gown would be close to the hearth so that in the house she went by the name of Cinderbreech ; but one of the girls who was not so rude as to call her by that name, gave her the name of Cinderella. And Cinderella, with all her dirt and rags, was ten times more sweet than her sisters, in all their fine clothes.

It came to pass that the King's son gave a ball to which he bade all who were rich and gay in the land : the two sisters of Cinderella were not left out, for the King's son did not know how rude and bad they were, but thought as they were so sweet and good when he saw them, that they must be so at all times. He did not ask Cinderella, for he had not seen her, nor heard of her. So the two girls went out to buy all they thought they should want to wear at the ball. They tried on the gowns and shoes, and things to wear on their heads, which they thought would look the best. All this was a new grief to poor Cinderella, for it was she who had to wash her sisters' fine clothes and lace, and wait on them. Their talk all the time was of how they should dress. " I," said one, " will wear my red silk, with French fringe." " And I," said her sister, "shall wear the same skirt I had made for the last ball ; but then, to make up for that, I shall put on my train with gold braid on it, and wear my pearls in my hair; with these I am sure to look well." They sent some miles for the girl who knew best how to dress the hair, and all the things they wore were bought at the best shops. The sisters did not eat for two days, so great was their joy as the day drew near. On the day of the ball they let Cinderella come up stairs to talk with them of their dress, for they knew she had a great deal of taste. Cinderella told them what she thought would look well, and said that if they would let her, she would help them to dress. This was just the thing to suit them, and so they let her do it. As she did all she could to aid her sisters, they said to her, "Cinderella, should not you like to go to the ball?" "Ah," said Cinderella, "do not laugh at me; it is not for such as I am to think that I may go to balls." "You are in the right," said they; "folks might well laugh to see a Cinderbreech dance in a ball-room." Some girls in Cinderella's place would have tried to make the proud girls dress in a way that would not look well, but, far from that, the sweet girl did all she could think of to make them look well. Cinderella broke more than twelve strings, as she tried to lace them so as to give them a fine shape, and they stood all the time in front of the glass. At length the day of the ball came, and the proud girls got in a fine coach. Next to the coach came two or three men in fine clothes to wait on them, and so they drove to where the prince dwelt. Cinderella stood at the door to watch them as long as she could see them, and when they were out of sight, she sat down on the door step and cried. Her godmother, who saw her in tears, bade her tell her what made her cry. " I wish,— I w-i-s-h," said poor Cinderella with a sob, but she could not say a word more. The godmother, who was a fairy, said to her, " You wish to go to the ball, Cinderella ;

is not this the truth?" "Ah, yes," said the poor child, and she gave one more sob. "Well, well, be a good girl," said the godmother, "and you shall go." She then led Cinderella to her room and said to her, "Run to the yard and bring me a gourd." Cinderella ran like the wind, and brought as big a one as she could lift. Her godmother took out the seeds, and left just the rind; she then struck it with her wand and the gourd was no more a gourd, but a fine coach with gold on the top and on all the sides of it. She then went to her mouse-trap, where she found six mice, none of whom were dead; she told Cinderella to lift up the door of the trap with great care, and as the mice went out she laid the end of her wand on them one by one, and each one took the form of a fine grey horse. "Here, my child," said the godmother, "is a coach and six, as fine as your sisters', but what shall we do for a man to drive?" "I will run," said Cinderella, "and see if there is not a rat in the trap; if there should be one, can he not drive?" "Well thought of, my child," said her godmother; " make what haste you can. Cinderella brought the rat-trap, which, to her great joy, had in it three large rats. The fairy chose the one which had the best beard ; she gave him a stroke with her wand, and in less time than you could say Jack Frost, he grew to be a fine tall man, with a beard so long that it hung down to his waist.   She next said to Cinderella, "Go back to the yard and you will find six snails, close by the well ; bring them here."   When this was done, with a stroke from the fairy's wand, they were six young men, who all gave a jump up to the back of the coach in their fine clothes, and stood side by side as well as if they had stood there the whole of their lives. The fairy then said to Cinderella, "Well, my dear, is not this such a coach as you

CINDERELLA.

would wish for to take you to the ball? Does it not please you?" "Yes, but,"—said Cinderella, and she could not go on. At last she said, " Must I go there in these rags?" Her godmother gave her a slight touch with the wand and she saw no more her rags, but a fine dress with a fringe of gold thread, and pearls as pure as can be found in the whole world. She gave her too a pair of glass slippers, and bade her go to the house of the Prince. The fairy,

when she took leave of Cinderella, told her by no means to stay
at the ball till the clock struck
twelve, for at twelve her coach
would change to a gourd, each
horse would change to a mouse,
the young men at the back of the
coach would be snails, and her
fine clothes would be rags. Cinderella said to her godmother, that
she would do all she told her to,
and, wild with joy, she drove to
the house of the Prince. As soon
as she got there, the King's son,

(who had been told that a great Princess, whom no one knew, was come to the ball) went to the door of her coach, gave her his hand to help her out, and led her to the ball-room. When Cinderella came in, all was still; for a while there was no dance, and the band did not play; all stood still to look at the fair girl whom no one knew. On all sides were heard the words, " How fair she is !" The King, old as he was, could not keep his eyes from her, and said all the time to the Queen that it was long since he had seen one so fair.

All who were at the ball tried to find out how her clothes were made, so that they might get some like them for the next day, if they should have the luck to meet with such rich stuffs to make them of, and girls who knew how to make them. The King's son took her to the best seat, and soon led her out to the dance with him. She could both walk and dance with so much grace that the eyes of all were on her still more than at first, and they thought no one in the world was so fair as she was, or could dance so well as she did. By and by a rich feast was brought up, but the young Prince did but look at her ; he could not eat. Cinderella sat near her sisters, and was so kind as to give them a part of the grapes and sweet things which the Prince gave her, while they, on their part, did not know what to make of these gifts from one whom they did not know.

As they ate the nice fruit, Cinderella saw by the clock that it
was near twelve. She rose from
her seat, said good bye to the
guests, and went out of the room
as fast as she could. As soon
as she got home she flew to her
godmother, gave her her best
thanks more than once, and told
her she would give the world to
go to the ball the next night, for
the King's son had said he would
like her to be there. When she
had told her godmother all she

had seen and done at the ball, the two sisters gave a loud knock at the door, so Cinderella went to let them in. " How late you are !" said she, and she gave a great yawn and put her hand up to her eyes to rub them, as if she had but just got up from her sleep, though she had in truth felt no wish for sleep since they had left her. If you had been at the ball, said one of the sisters, you could not have slept. No one in all the land has seen so fair a Princess as came to the ball this night; and she was so kind to us, and made us take a part of the grapes and sweet things which the Prince gave her. It was hard for Cinderella to hide her joy. She said to her sisters that she would like to know the name of this Princess, but they said that no one could find out who she was, which gave great grief to the King's son, so that he said he would pay a large sum to the man who would find out where she came from. Cinderella could not hide a smile, and said, "How fair she must be! Ah, how I wish I could see her, if it were but for one half hour! Dear Miss Ann, will you not lend me the gown you wear all the time at home, and let me go to see her?" "Oh yes, I guess so! lend my clothes to a Cinderbreech! Do you think me such a fool? No, no! pray Miss Pert, mind your own work, and leave dress and balls for those who are more fit for them than you are." Cinderella thought she would make some such speech as that, and it did not grieve her, for she would have been quite at a loss what to do, if her sister had lent her the clothes that she spoke of. The next night the sisters went once more to the ball, and so did Cinderella, but her dress was still more to her taste than the one she had on the first night of the ball. The King's son kept by her side all the time, and said to her all the sweet things he could think of. The fair young

girl did not tire of the joys of the
ball; no, far from that, she had so
much joy in them that she did not
once think of what her godmother
had told her. Cinderella at last
heard a clock strike; it struck one,
two, three, four, five, and so on
till it came to twelve, though she
felt sure it could not be so late.
She got up and flew like a deer
out of the ball-room. The Prince
tried to catch her, but poor Cinderella's fright made her run so
fast that he could not get near her.

But in her great haste she let fall one of her glass slippers ; the Prince made one of the men whose place it was to wait on him stoop down and pick it up and give it to him, and he took great care of it. Cinderella got home quite out of breath, in her old clothes, with no coach, no men to drive or stand at the back of the coach, and no trace of her fine clothes left but one glass slipper, like the one she had let fall. In the mean while the Prince did not fail to ask all the guards at the doors of his house if they had not seen a grand Princess pass out, and which way she went. The guards said that no Princess had gone through the doors, and that they had seen no one but a girl all in rags, who did not look fit to beg, much less to be a Princess. When the two sisters came back from the ball, Cinderella thought she would ask them if they had found it as gay as they did the first night, and if the fair Princess had been

there. They told her that she had,
but as soon as the clock struck
twelve she ran from the ball-room,
and in the great haste she made, she
had let fall one of her glass slippers,
which was as small as could be ;
that the King's son had found it,
and had done naught else all the
rest of the night but sit still and
look at it, and that all thought he
was much in love with the fair
Princess who had let it fall. This
was the truth ; for when a few
days had gone by, the Prince made

it known that he would take for
his wife the girl whose foot would
just fit the slipper he had found.
So he sent out some of his men,
who took the slipper and went
first to all the Princesses ; then
to the next in rank, in short they
went to all at the court, but found
no one who could wear the
slipper. They then brought it
to the two sisters, who each tried
all she could to put her foot in the
slipper, but saw at last that it
could not be done. Cinderella all

the while stood by and saw all that was done; she knew her slipper, and could not hide a smile as she said, " Pray, sir, let me try to get on the slipper." He made her sit down, and put the slipper to her foot. It went on with ease, and he saw that it was just the right size. The two sisters did not know what to think when they saw that the slipper was the right size for Cinderella, but who can tell what they felt, when she drew from her work bag the mate to it, and put it on.

Just then the fairy came in. She
gave Cinderella a touch with her
wand, and in place of her rags was
seen the dress she had worn the last
night she was in the Prince's house.
The two sisters then saw that she
was the fair Princess they had
seen at the ball. They fell at her
feet to beg her to think no more
of their rude acts and cross words.
Cinderella bade them rise and
gave them each a kiss with much
love. She said that she would
think no more of what they had

done if they would but love her.
Cinderella was then led, in her gay
dress, to the young Prince, who
found her as fair and good as he
thought her the two nights he saw
her at the ball ; so he said she
should be his wife ; this came to
pass in few a days, and as she was
as good as she was fair, she gave her
sisters fine rooms in the house of
the Prince, and soon they were
the wives of two great lords of
the Court.

THE FAIR ONE WITH THE GOLDEN LOCKS.

THERE was once a fair and good Princess, whose name was The Fair One with Locks of Gold, for her hair shone as gold shines, and fell in curls down to her feet. On her head she wore all the time a bright wreath. This wreath was made with first a white rose and then a red rose, and so on, and with them pearls and rich gems of all kinds. A rich young King whose

land lay next to hers, and who
had heard how fair she was, fell
in love with her, though he had not
seen her, and sent to ask if she
would be his wife. The man who
was sent to ask her if she would
be the wife of the King, wore a
rich dress, and with him went
ten men to wait on him, each of
whom sat on a fine horse. The
King, who had made up his mind
that he would have the Princess
for his wife, told the man who was
sent to ask her, to say all the kind

things he could think of to please
her, and he had great hopes that
he would bring the Princess back
with him ; but it might be that
that day she did not feel well, or
that she did not like the things
that were said to her, I do not
know which ; but she told the man
to thank the King for his kind
wish, and say that she had no mind
to be a wife at all. When the man
got back to the King's chief town,
where the King stood near the
gate to watch for him, the men of

the land felt great grief to see that he had come back and had not brought with him the Fair One with Locks of Gold, and the King wept like a child.

There was a youth at Court who was as fair and bright as the sun. There was no one at Court who had so fine a form or who knew so much as he, and for his grace and wit, they gave him the name of Avenant, which means, full of grace and wit. The King was fond of him ,and in truth all men were fond of him, but those who had bad hearts, and who could not bear to see the good young man have more of the King's love than they had. As Avenant took a walk one day with some men, he said, and did not wait to think if it was a wise thing to say : " If the King had sent me to the Fair One with Locks of Gold, I dare say I could have said some things that would have made her come back with me." These men, who in their hearts did not wish

Avenant good luck, ran as fast as they could go, to the King, and said, "Sir, sir, do you know what Avenant says? He boasts that if you sent him to the Fair One with the Locks of Gold, he could have brought her with him, which shows he is so vain as to think that his face is as fine as your own, and that her love for him would have made her go with him to the end of the world." Then the King flew in a great rage. "What!" said he, "does this young scamp make a jest at my bad luck, and think that he could do more than I could? Go as fast as you can, and put him in a dark cell, and there let him starve to death." The King's guards went at once to seize Avenant, who thought no more of what he had said, took him to a dark cell, and put on him such chains as they would have put on a wild beast. One day, when his strength was well nigh spent, he gave a deep sigh, and then cried out, "What wrong can the King think I have done? There is not a man in all the land who is more true to him than I am, and all I have done in my whole life has been with a view to please him." The King by chance stood just then close by the door of his cell, and he stood still to hear him, though those that were with the King tried to talk so loud that he could not hear Avenant, and did not wish to let him stop. " Hold your peace," said the King, " and let me hear him out." When he had done so, he felt sad to think that Avenant, whom he had been fond of, should be in so much grief, so he went to the door of the cell, and spoke to him, and he made the man who had the key of the cell let Avenant out. So he came forth in a sad plight, and fell on his knees at the King's feet; "What have I done, sir," said he, "that you should thus load me with grief and pain?" Thou hast made fun of me, and of the man whom I sent to the Fair One with

the Locks of Gold, and hast said
that if I had sent thee to her, thou
couldst have brought her with
thee." "It is true, sir," said Avenant, "for I would have told her
of all the things that are great and
good in you, and then she could
not have had the heart to say no
to me, and all the things I said to
her I would in truth have said in
your name, and not in my own"
Now that Avenant had had a
chance to tell the King what he
meant, the King found he had

done no wrong, so he bade him
leave his cell and come with him,
for his kind heart was quite sad to
to think of the wrong he had done
him. The King told his men to
give Avenant a good meal, for he
was faint for want of food, and
then he sent for him to come to
his room. " Avenant," said he,
" I still love the Fair One with
Locks of Gold. I have a mind to
send thee to her, to try if thou
canst get her for me." Avenant
said that he was glad to do all

things that the King told him, and would set out the next day at dawn. " Hold," said the King, " I will give thee a fine horse and twelve men to go with thee and wait on thee." " There is no need of that," said Avenant; " I want naught but a good horse, and a note from you to let the Princess see that it is you that have sent me ." Then the King gave him a kiss, he was so glad to hear that he would set out so soon.

It was on the third day of the
week that he took leave of the
King and his friends.   He left the
King's house at break of day, and
soon he came to a large field.   As
he rode through it, a fine thought
came to his mind ; so he got off
his horse, and sat down by the
bank of a small stream, that ran
on one side of the field, and wrote
the thought down in a small book
that he had with him.   When he
had done so, he gave a good look
round him on all sides, for there

were charms for him in the fair
scene that met his eyes; all at
once he saw a large carp, that
shone like gold.   It shook its
head, and that was all it could do,
for it had tried to catch some small
flies, and, as it did so, it gave a
leap so far out of the stream, as to
fall on the grass, where it was well
nigh dead, for it could not live on
the land, and could not get back to
the stream.   Avenant thought he
would help the poor thing, and
though it was a fish day, and he

would have been glad to take it
with him and cook it to eat at noon,
he took it up and put it with care
in the stream, where the carp, as
it felt the cool stream, grew well
and strong and felt quite gay. It
went down to the stones and mud
on which the stream ran ; but soon
it came up once more, brisk and
gay to the side of the stream. " Avenant," said the carp, " I thank you
for the kind act you have done to
me ; had it not been for you, I had
died ; but you have been so good

as to save my life, and I will pay
you for it, when you need my help.
The next day, as he still went on
his way, he saw a crow in great
fear, for close to it he saw a huge
bird of prey, which would soon
have come up with it and put an
end to its life. He took his bow,
which he had at all times with him
when he was out of doors, and took
aim at the bird of prey ; he let fly
a shaft which hit him in the heart
so that he fell down dead. When
the crow saw this, it came and sat

on a tree near Avenant, half wild
with joy. "Avenant," said the
crow, "you have been kind, (more
kind than most men are,) to help
me, who am but a poor, black
crow ; but I will not cease to think
of what you have done, and one
day will do you as good a turn."
Avenant was struck with the sense
of the crow, but thought no more
of what he had done, and went on
his way. One day, when it was
not yet dawn, he came to a thick
wood ; it was so dark that it was

hard for him to find his way, and
there he heard the voice of an owl,
who cried out as if in great pain
or grief. He gave a look round
him on all sides and at last came
to a place where some boys had
spread their nets in the night time,
to catch poor birds. " What a
shame it is !" said he, "men seem
to be made each one to tease the
rest as much as he can, or else to kill
poor dumb things that can do them
no harm !" When he had said this
he took out his knife, cut the cords

and let the owl go free ; but as it flew off, it said, " Avenant, the boys, who would have put an end to my life are close at hand, they would have caught me and I must have died, if you had not come to save my life. I have a heart full of thanks for what you have done, and will not cease to think of it, as long as I live." These three things were all that were strange, while Avenant was on his way, and when he got to the place it was his aim to reach

he took a bath, and put on a suit
of cloth of gold.   When he had
done this, he put a scarf with rich
work on it, round his neck, and
took in his arms a small dog that
he was quite fond of.   And Avenant was so good and kind,
and all that he did was done with
so good a grace, that when he
stood at the gate of the Fair One's
house, all the guards took off their
hats to him, and all strove to see
who should be the first to tell the
Fair One with Locks of Gold,

that Avenant, a man sent by the
King, whose land was next to hers,
had come to her house to see and
speak with her. When the Fair
One with Locks of Gold heard
the name of Avenant, she said,
" It has a sweet sound, and I dare
say he is as good as his name, and
all who know him love him ;" and
she said to her maids, who at all
times stood near her, " Go, bring
me my gown of blue silk, with rich
work of gold thread on it ; dress
my hair, and bring me my wreaths ;

let each rose be fresh and pure,
just from the bush ; let me have
my high shoes and my fan ; and
let my room, where I see those
who have things of great weight
to say, and my throne, be clean,
and on them rich cloths ; for I
would have him say with truth
through all the land, that I am in
fact, what men say I am, the Fair
One with Locks of Gold.   Thus
all her maids were soon at work
to dress her as a Queen should be.
At length she went to a room

where there was a glass at each end, and one at each side ; there she stood and gave a look to see if her dress was as it should be, and if there were no more things she could put on to make her look well; then she went up to her throne of gold and rare wood from the far East, the sweet smell of which was like the sweet smell of the best of balm. She told her maids, too, to take their harps and play and sing their sweet songs, so that no one could fail to be pleased.

Avenant was then led to the
room where the Fair One with the
Locks of Gold sat on her throne,
and he stood there, so wild with
joy to see so fair a sight that, as
he told his friends when he got
home, at first he could not move
his lips to say what he came there
for. But at last he took heart and
made his speech with much grace.
In this speech the last thing he
said was to beg the Princess not to
let him have the bad luck to go
back, and not take her with him.

"Young Avenant," said she, "all that you have said is good, and well said, and I had as lief go with you and be the wife of your King, as stay here and reign in my own land ; but you must know that four or five weeks since, I went to take the air by the side of a stream, with my maids who wait on me ; as I took off my glove, there came off with it a ring that I wore night and day, and this ring fell in the stream and was lost. This ring I care more for than for my land and

my throne, so you can judge how
sad I am to think I have lost it;
and I have made a vow that I will
not be the wife of a man, though
he be a rich and great king, if the
man who comes to ask me, will
not bring me my ring.   This is
the gift which you have to make
me, and if you do not do so, you
may talk your heart out, for though
months and years may pass I will
not draw back from what I have
said."   When he got back to the
place where he slept at night, he

did not stay to take his tea, but went to bed with a sad heart; and the small dog that he had with him, whose name was Cabriole, like him, would take no food, but went and lay down by his side. Avenant spent the night in sighs and groans and tears, and said, "How can I find a ring that fell in a great stream more than a month since. All men would say that I had not the least sense, if I did but try to find it. The Fair One with Locks of Gold, when she gave me this task, knew that no man could do such a thing, and that is why she told me to do it." His sighs and groans grew worse ; Cabriole saw this and said, " Dear Avenant, you, who at all times are so good and kind to me, and whom I will serve as long as I live, pray do not give up all hope ; you will not lose your good luck, for you are too good a man to fail in what you try to do ; so when it is day, let us go to the side of the stream." Avenant did not say a word, but gave his dog two or three slight taps with his hand, and as he was worn out with grief, he at last went to sleep. But when Cabriole saw that it was broad day, he gave such a loud bark that the young man woke. " Rise, sir," said he ; "put on your clothes and let us go and try what luck we shall have." Avenant thought that what his small dog said was wise, so he got up, put on his clothes and went down to the yard, and then he went out of the yard to the side of the stream. He did not mean to go there, for he thought there was no hope that he should find the ring, but he went on with his hat low down on his eyes, and his hands at his back, and thought that all he had to do now was to take his leave, and go back to his King, when all at once he heard a voice call, "Avenant! Avenant!" which made him look round; but as he saw no one, he made up his mind that it could not have been his name that he heard, and so he went on his way ; but soon he once more heard a voice call him. " Who calls me ?" said he. Cabriole, who was close to the stream, gave a look in, and cried out. " Oh Avenant, look here ; the voice comes from a carp that shines like gold." Then the carp came up to the top of the stream, and with a voice that was so loud that it could be heard twelve yards off, said, " Avenant, you were so good as to save my life, down in the field of oaks, where I must have died, if it had not been for your help, and now I am come to pay you for that kind deed. Here, my dear Avenant, here is the ring which the Fair One with the Locks of Gold let fall in the stream." So Avenant bent down to the stream and took the ring out of the carp's mouth, and gave him his best thanks. And now he felt that he need not take his leave, he went straight to the gate of the house where the Fair One with Locks of Gold had her home.

He took with him his small dog, Cabriole, who did not cease to skip and jump and wag his tail for joy that he had made Avenant walk by the side of the stream. When the Fair One was told that Avenant would like to speak to her, " Ah," said she, "the poor youth has come to take his leave of me. He has thought that what I told him to do, can not be done, and he will go back to his King." But Avenant, when they let him in, went up to the throne, on which

she sat, and gave her the ring.
As he did so, he said, "Fair One,
see, I have done what you told me,
and now I hope you will let the
King, who sent me here, take you
for his wife." When she saw her
ring, and that no harm was done
to it, she did not know how
to think that her eyes told her the
truth. "I am sure, young man,"
said she, "some fairy must have
come to your aid, for if you had
not some such help, this could not
have been done." "Fair One,"

said he, " I know no fairy, but I had the will to do what you told me to." " Well, then, since you have so good a will," she went on to say, " there are more things that you can do for me, and if you do not do them I will not be a wife.

" There is a great Prince, who lives not far from here, whose name is Galifron, and who will not rest at ease, if I do not let him make me his wife. He told me his mind with harsh threats that

if I said no to him, he would come
to my land with fire and sword,
but you shall judge if I could be
the wife of such a man ; he is as
tall as the spire of a church ; he
eats up men as an ape eats nuts ;
when he goes through his land, he
takes great ten inch guns in his
hands to fire in place of the small
guns that most men use; and
when he speaks out loud, it makes
the ears of those that are near him
quite deaf.   I told him that I did
not choose to be a wife, and when

I said that I was in hopes that he would ask me no more. But he does not cease to write and ask me to be his wife ; he has put my men to the sword, and he has slain crowds of them ; so if you wish me to go with you to your King, you must first fight him and bring me his head." Avenant gave a start when he heard this, but when he had thought of it for a while, he said, " Well, ma'am, I will fight this Galifron ; I think that he will slay me, but I will die like a man who is proud to lose his life, if, when he does so, he can serve his King and the land of his birth." When the Fair One with Locks of Gold had heard his bold words, she thought still more of him than she had done, and could not bear to have him slain; so she said all she could to keep him from such a sad fate, but it was all in vain, for he would go; he had made up his mind that he would win her for his King. At last he came to the strong fort where Galifron was.

The roads all the way to it were strewn with the bones of the men whom this vile wretch had cut to bits, or made a meal of. In a short time, Avenant saw the huge man come near, and it did not take him long to tell him that he would fight him, but there was no need for this, for Galifron took up his great mace, made of steel, and would have beat out the brains of young Avenant at the first blow, but a crow just then took her seat on Galifron's head, and it took

her but a short time to peck out
both his eyes ; the blood ran
down his face, which made him
wild with rage, and he struck
with his mace on all sides, but
Avenant took care to keep out of
the way of his blows, and gave
him some great wounds with his
sword, which he did not fail to
put in him, quite up to the hilt, so
that in half an hour the wretch
grew faint and fell to the ground,
with loss of blood. Avenant then
cut off his head, and while he was

so wild with joy that he did not
know what to do, the crow flew to
a tree and stood on a limb near
him, and said, " Avenant, the kind
act that you did has not gone out
of my mind. You slew the bird
of prey that would have put an
end to my life. I told you that I
would pay you for it, and now I
have been as good as my word."
"You have, in truth, been kind,
Miss Crow," said Avenant, "I
now owe you my life, and shall be
glad at all times to do you a good

turn if I can." When he had said this, he got on his horse and rode off with the huge head of the man he had slain. When he came to the town, all the world ran to him and cried out, " Long live the brave Avenant, who has slain the man whom no one else could slay!" So that the Fair One, who heard the noise, and shook with fear. lest she should hear of the death of young Avenant, durst not ask what was the cause of the noise. But soon she saw

FAIR ONE WITH GOLDEN LOCKS.

Avenant come in with the huge head in his arms ; when she saw the huge head she once more shook with fear, though now there was no cause for it. " Fair One," said he, " you see that he who would have made you his wife by force, and come to your land with fire and sword, is dead, and you have no more to fear from him. Now I hope you will cease to say no to the King who sent me here." "Ah," said the Fair One with Locks of Gold, " I must still say no to him, if you can not find means to fill me a vase from the spring in the Cave of Gloom. Not far from here," she went on to say, " there is a deep cave, five or six leagues round; the door to it is kept by two fierce dragons. The dragons dart fire from their mouths and eyes, and when you have got through the door of this cave, you will meet with a deep hole: down this hole you must go, and you will find it full of worms and snails and toads and snakes.

Deep in this hole there is a kind of vault, and through this vault there runs a spring, the name of which is the Spring of Health. The vase which I will give you, you must fill at the spring; the things that it can do are most strange. Those who are fair, when they wash with it, do not cease to be so, and those who are not so, grow fair at once; if they are young, it keeps them young ; and if they are old, it brings back their youth. Now judge you, Avenant, if I

will leave my land, if some man
will not first take a vase and fill it
for me at that spring." " Ma'am,"
said he, " you are so fair that you
need no aid of this kind ; but I see
that though I have been sent to
you by a good and great king, you
seek my death.   Yet I will go in
search of what you ask, though it
is a sure thing that I shall come
back no more." At length he
came to the top of a high hill,
where he sat down to rest, for it
was a warm day and he had made

all the haste he could. He let go the rein of his horse that he might feed, and Cabriole ran from place to place, to try to catch flies.

He knew that the Cave of Gloom was not far off, and he gave a good look on all sides to see if he could find it, and at length he saw a huge rock as black as ink, whence there came out a thick smoke, and just then he saw one of the dragons, who cast forth fire from his jaws and eyes; his skin on his back was blue and green, and on his sides red as blood. He had great claws, and a long tail which he could roll up in ten times ten folds.

Avenant made up his mind that he would fight him and die. He drew his sword, and with the vase in his hand which the Fair One with Locks of Gold gave him to fill at the Spring of Health, he drew near to the cave, and as he did so he said to his small dog, " Cabriole, here is an end of me. I can not fill this vase at the spring;

the dragons guard it with too much care. So when I am dead, fill this vase with my blood and take it to the Fair One that she may see what this hard thing that she bade me do has cost me. Then go to the King who sent me here, and tell him of all the bad luck that has come to me." When he had said this he heard a voice call " Avenant! Avenant!" "Who calls me ;" said he, and soon he saw an owl in a hole in the trunk of an old tree ; as he stood still to

look, he heard the owl call his
name once more, and then it said,
" You were so kind as to save me,
when the bad boys had laid a snare,
and meant to kill me for their
sport.   I should have lost my life
had it not been for you : I told you
I would pay you for it, and now
the time is come for me to do so ;
I know all the ways in and out of
the Cave of Gloom ; give me your
vase, and I will go and fill it for
you at the Spring of Health."
Avenant was most glad to give

him the vase, and the owl went to the cave; no one could keep out the owl, for it flew up high, so that the dragons could not reach it, so it went in, and in less than half an hour it came out with the vase quite full. Avenant was full of joy at his good luck; he gave the owl his best thanks for what he had done for him, and went back, with a gay heart, to the town. When he got there he went straight to the house of the Fair One with Locks of Gold, and

gave her the vase ; so then
she could no more say that she
would not go with Avenant.   She
gave Avenant her thanks, and told
her maids to pack up all the things
that she would need to go to the
land of Avenant's King ; then they
set out on their way.   As they
went on, the Fair One with
Locks of Gold found that Avenant was as wise and good as he
was brave, and said to him more
than once on the road, " If it had
been your wish, I could have made

you a King, and then we need
not have left my land." But when
she said such things, Avenant said
to her, " I would not have done so
great a wrong to my King, whom
I serve, though it might have
brought me all the lands of the
earth. Yet I must say that you
are more fair and bright than the
sun." At length they came to the
chief town of the King, who, when
he heard that the Fair One with
Locks of Gold had come, went
forth to meet her, and made her

rich gifts of all the fine things in
the world. they were wed mid
feasts and balls and loud shouts of
joy, from all the folks in the land,
so that no one could talk of aught
but them. But the Fair One with
Locks of Gold had great love for
Avenant in her heart, and felt no
joy when he did not chance to be
with her. She spoke at all times
in his praise. " I should not have
come here," said she to the King,
" had it not been for Avenant, who,
to serve me, found a ring which I

had let fall in a stream where no
one else could find it; he slew a
huge man whom no one else
would dare to go near, and there
is one thing more for which you
owe him thanks. I sent him to a
spring which no one else could
get at, to fill for me a vase, by
means of which I shall keep, all my
life, as fair and in as good health
as I am now." The men with bad
hearts who could not bear to see
the good luck of Avenant, and who
heard the Queen's words, said to

the King one day, " Sir, if you had
not the best of hearts, you would
see the wrong that the Queen and
Avenant do you, for she is in love
with him with her whole heart."
" Is that so ?" said the King.   " In
fact, now that I think of it, I see
the truth of what you have told
me.   Let him be put in a dark
cell, with chains on his feet and
hands."   So they laid hands on
Avenant at once and took him to a
dark cell.   On his hands and feet
they put chains of such weight

that he could scarce move. But his small dog Cabriole did not leave him, but did the best he could to cheer him, and brought him all the news of the court. When the Fair One with Locks of Gold heard of his sad fate, she fell down at the King's feet, and, all in tears, tried to get him to let Avenant out of his cell. But the more she tried to move the King the more his rage grew, for he thought that she felt more love for Avenant than for him, and that it

was this love that made her beg
so hard for him to be let out.
When she found she could not
gain her end, she said no more to
him, but she grew day by day
more sad.   The King took it in
his head that she did not think
him as fair as Avenant, so he
thought he would wash his face
with what was in the vase that
the Queen had sent by Avenant
to the Spring of Health, in her
own land, in hopes that the Queen
would then feel more love for him

than she had done so far. This
vase stood on a stand in the room
of the Queen, where she had put it
that it might not be out of her
sight. But one of the maids
whose place it was to sweep that
room, tried to kill a fly with her
short broom, and by chance threw
down the vase, so that all that was
in it ran out. She dried it up
with all the speed she could, and
at first she did not know what to
do, but it came her mind to that
she had seen in the King's room a

jar of some kind of clear stuff,
that was just like what she had
spilt. So with no more loss of
time, she went and got the jar,
and put in the vase as much as
it had in it when she had the bad
luck to throw it down, and then
put the jar back in its place. Now
this stuff which was in the King's
room, was a kind of drug, which
he made use of to kill the great
lords and dukes of his court, when
he found that they had done some
great crime. He did not wish a

lord or duke to be hung, or have his head cut off, so he made him rub his face with this drug, which put him to sleep, a sleep so deep that he woke no more on earth. Now the King, who thought he would like to grow fair, one night took up the vase, and for half an hour did not cease to rub his face with the drug. At the end of that time he went to sleep and died. Cabriole was one of the first who found out what had come to pass, and ran with all speed to tell Av-

enant of it, who bade him go to
the Fair One with Locks of Gold
and ask her if she still thought of
his chains and his dark cell. Cabriole went with all the haste he
could through the crowd ; no one
saw him, for there was a great
noise and stir at court, when they
found that the King was dead ; he
soon made his way to the Queen.
" Ma'am," said he, " Do you
think no more of poor Avenant?"
This brought to her mind all that
the poor youth had borne for her

sake, and what he had done for her. She did not say a word, but went straight to the dark cell, and took off the chains from Avenant's hands and feet with her own fair hands; then she put the crown on his head, and threw the King's cloak round him. "Dear Avenant," said she, "I will make you a great Prince, and take you for my spouse." Avenant fell down at her feet, and in terms of great love gave her his thanks. All the men in the land were glad to have

him for their King. They were
wed with great feasts and balls,
such as had not been seen till then
in all the world; and the Fair
One with Locks of Gold, had the
good luck to live a long time with
her dear Avenant, and they both
had naught but peace and joy to
the end of their lives.

GOODY TWO SHOES.

ALL the world must have heard of Goody Two Shoes, for this young girl grew to be so well known, that more than one man has tried to write her life. And her tale has not been at all times told the same way, by the men who told or wrote it. She was born in a land that is not on this side of the sea ; but in that land, as in this, the laws are as just and good to the poor man, as to the

man who is rich and great, and
has as much gold as he knows
what to do with ; and the poor
man who lives in a low hut by the
way side, is just as free as the
sons of the King. The true name
of this young girl, whom we call
Goody Two Shoes, was Madge
Meanwell. Her father had a
small farm, not far from the town
of Mouldwell, and at one time he
was quite well off. But it was
the will of God that his lot should
be a sad one. Things went wrong

on the farm, he grew poor, and was, at last, quite in want. The farm of poor Mr. Meanwell was sold to pay those to whom he was in debt, for he was too good a man to keep a farm, which, now, it would not be right to call his own. Those to whom he was in debt, thought well of him when they saw him part with all that he had to pay all the debts he could, and they took what part of their claims he could give them, and and did not find fault, and scold,

that he could not pay them quite
all he owed.   That is to say, they
all did so but one ; that one was
Sir Thomas Gripe, who had great
wealth but not a kind heart ; in
short, he was one of those men
who grab all they can get, and
will not part with a cent to help
those who are in need.   He made
up his mind that he would go to
law with poor Meanwell, and get
what was due to him, or else
have him shut up in a cell where
in those days they kept those who

did not pay their debts. Poor Meanwell, to keep out of the way of this man with a hard heart, left the land of his birth, and with his wife and boy and girl, went to a strange land. There no one knew what a good and true man he was, so no one would give him work; to make things worse, he caught a bad cold, for want of clothes to keep him warm; this, with the grief and care he felt as he thought of the sad lot of those who were most dear to him, was soon the cause of his death. When his poor wife saw that he was dead it broke her heart ; she did not live more than two days more, and then died and left Madge and her young brother Tom to the wide world. When their mother was dead it would have done your heart good to see how fond the girl was of the boy, and the boy of her. They were rich in love, but they were poor in all things else, and as they had no father or mother, or friends to take care of them, they were all in rags ; as for Tom, he had two shoes, but Madge had but one. For some days they had no food to eat but some fruit that they got from the hedge at the side of the road, and a few crusts of bread that some poor folks gave them, and at night they lay down and slept in a barn. They had some great aunts, but these great aunts would not speak to them ; no, they were rich, and too proud to own a poor girl like Madge, all in rags, or a small boy like Tom, whose curls hung down on his face, with no aid from brush or comb, and whose clothes were by no means free from dirt. The friends of some folks will not speak to them when they are poor, but when they get rich they grow fond of them, and this will at all times be the case with those who love gold more than true worth. But such bad folks, who love naught but gold, and are proud and do not care for the poor, are not apt to

come to a good end, as we shall
see by and by.

Mr. Smith was a good priest,
whose home was in the town
where Madge was born, but as he
had but a small church, from
which he did not get much pay,
he could not do as his heart bade
him, and help all those whom he
knew were in need of help. As
he had known Mr. Meanwell,
when he had his farm and was
quite rich, he would have been glad
to be of use to his poor boy and

girl, who now had no father or mother to take care of them. It came to pass that a friend of his came to see him, who was a good kind man, and Mr. Smith, by his wish, sent for the boy and girl to come to him. The kind man said that Madge should have a new pair of shoes, and he gave her some gold to buy clothes, and said he would take Tom and send him to sea, so he had nice new clothes made for him. When some days had gone by, this kind man went back to the great town he had come from, and took with him Tom, of whom you will know more by and by ; for we shall at a fit time tell you some of the things that came to pass in his life. When this boy and girl had to part, it was in truth a sad sight. Tom cried and Margery cried, and she gave him a kiss more than ten times, and he did the same thing to her. At last Tom tried to wipe off her tears with the end of his coat, and bade her cry no more, for that he

would come to see her as soon as
he got back from sea. When
night came, poor Madge grew full
of grief and care, as she thought
of Tom, and when she had sat up
as late as Mr. Smith would let her,
she went to bed to cry there.
Poor Margery got up at dawn the
next day, and ran all round the
town and cried for Tom, and
when some hours had gone by,
she came back with a heart full of
grief. But just then, the man who
made shoes, came in with the new

shoes, that the kind friend of Mr. Smith had told him to make to fit her. I do not know what could have made poor Madge bear the great grief she was in, if it had not been for the joy she had in her new shoes. She ran out to Mrs. Smith as soon as they were put on, and held up her frock so that she could see the shoes, and cried out, " Two shoes, Ma'am, see! two shoes." And she did the same thing to all the folks she met, and by that means she got

the name of Goody Two Shoes.
But the young girls of the town,
who at times came to play with
her, though it fun to call her old
Goody Two Shoes. Mr. and
Mrs. Smith would have been
quite glad, if they had been rich,.
to keep poor Madge for their
own child; but as they found
that they could not do that, they
had to trust her to God. As
Madge had seen how good, and
how wise, Mr. Smith was, she
thought the cause of it must be

that he knew so much more than the rest of the men in the town. So she took it in her head, that, more than all things, she would like to learn to read. But in those days there were no schools at the church, on the first day of the week, for girls to go to. So at first she was much at a loss to know how to learn; but at last she made up her mind to ask Mr. Smith to be so good as to teach her, when he had time. He said he would be quite glad to do so, and so Madge went to him for one hour each morn, for he had no more time than that to spare. By this means she soon came to know more than the girls she went to play with, and she made a plan to teach those who knew less than she did. This was the plan: Now that she knew her *a*, *b*, *c*, she found how few such signs we need to read and spell; for there are but twice ten and six to spell all the words in the world; but as some of these

are large and some small, she cut
out of a thin piece of wood ten
sets of each. Then she got an
old book, the first that Mr. Smith
gave her when he taught her to
spell, and made the girls set up
all the words they said they would
like to spell, and when they could
make words with ease, she taught
them to make a phrase. You
know what a phrase is my dear :
" I will be good," is a phrase, and
is made up of some words. The
way they had to spell, or play the

game was this : If they had to
spell mince pie, which is quite a
good thing, the girls all stood in
a ring, and the first girl brought an
m, the next girl brought an *i*, the
next an *n*, the next a *c*, the next an *e*,
and so on, till it was all done, and
if one girl brought an *m* when she
should have brought an *n*, or some
such wrong thing as that, she had
to pay a fine, or play no more.
This made them learn while they
were at their play, and each morn
she went round to teach the girls,

with her *a, b, c*'s in a box. I once
went the rounds with her and
thought it was great fun. The
first house we came to was Mr.
Wilson's; he had a fine farm of his
own. Here Madge meant to stop;
so she ran to the door. Tap,
tap, tap! "Who's there?" "No
one but Goody Two Shoes," said
Madge; "I have come to teach
Billy." "Oh Goody, dear," says
Mrs. Wilson, with joy in her face,
"I am glad to see you; it will
please Billy to hear that you have

come, for he knows quite well the words you gave him to learn." Then out came the small boy. " How do, Doody Two Shoes?" said he, for he could not speak plain. So she went in, as was her wont, and gave him some new words to learn. When we had left Mr. Wilson's, the next place we came to was Mr. Simpson's ; he too had a fine farm. " Bow, wow, wow !" said the dog. " Sir," said Mr. Wilson's wife, " why do you bark at Goody Two Shoes?

Come in, Madge ; here, Sally is in great need of you; she knows all her *a, b, c.*" When she had heard Sally say her *a, b, c* off she went to Mr. Cook's house. Here some poor boys and girls were met to learn, who all came round Madge, so she took out her bits of wood, and said to a small boy who stood close to her, " What did you have to eat at noon to day?" He said " Bread." " Then we will spell it," she said ; " what must you put up first?" He put up the *B ;* then the boy who stood next put up an *r*, the next *e*, the next *a*, the next *d*, and that was bread. " And what did you eat for lunch to day, Polly Gomb?" " Plum pie," said the girl, who was quite small ; so the one next in turn set up a great *P*, and the next an *l*, the next a *u*, and so on till the words Plum and Pie were set up side by side, and stood thus——Plum Pie. As she went through the town, she met with some bad boys who had got a · large black bird which they meant to throw stones at. She thought she would like to get the poor thing out of their rough hands, so she gave them two cents for him and brought him home. She gave him the name of Ralph, and a fine bird he was. And she thought how Noah, in the days of the flood, had sent out a large black bird, like this, to see if the flood was dried up on the face of the earth. And then she thought how our Lord, when he was on earth, spoke of birds, and said

" The fox has his hole, and the birds of the air have their nests, but the Son of Man hath not where to lay his head." Now this bird was one of those that can be taught to speak ; so she taught it to speak, to spell, and to read ; and as he was quite fond of the bits of wood that the girls and boys had to spell with, they used to call this Ralph's A, B, C.

A, B, C, D, E, F, G,
H, I, J, K, L, M, N,

O, P, Q, R, S, T, U, V, W, X, Y, Z.

When she had the big, black bird for some days, as she took a walk in the fields, she saw some bad boys, who had caught a dove, and tied a string to its legs, so as to let it fly and then draw it back when they chose ; and by this means they gave the poor bird the hope that it might get free, and then gave him a pull back to show him that they did not mean to let him go. She bought this dove too, and taught him how to spell and read, though not to talk ; and he did all those strange things which are told of the bird, well known to fame, who some time since was shown in all the large towns, and whom all the great men of the land came to see. This dove was a fine large bird, and she gave him the name of Tom. And as Black Ralph was fond of the large bits of wood, Tom the dove took care of the

small ones, of which he made this
a, *b*, *c*.

a, b, c, d, e, f, g, h, i, j, k, l, m, n,
o, p, q, r, s, t, u, v, w, x, y, z.

Mrs. Williams, who kept a school
to teach young folks how to say
their A, B, C, was at this time
quite old, and some days she felt
too weak to teach, so she said she
would like to give up this great
trust.   When this was told to Sir
William Dove, he told Mrs. Williams to talk to Goody Two Shoes

and see how much she knew
for he thought it might be that
she could teach in her place.
This was done, and Mrs. Williams spoke quite well of her;
what she said of her was this:
" That Madge, though she was
still quite small, knew more than
all the young girls she had had in
her school, and had the best head
and heart of them all. All who
were in the town thought well of
Mrs. Williams, and when they
had heard what she said, it made

them think well of Miss Madge,
for so we must now call her.
Miss Madge thought that this was
the best part of her life ; but there
was more joy yet in store for her.
The great and good God heaps
up rich gifts on all those who love
Him, and though for a time He
may let them be poor and in need,
and hide the good things that He
means to do for them from the
sight of men, yet in the end He
will crown them with joy, it may
be on this earth, and no one can

doubt that they are so in the bright world to come. As soon as she came to her new school, she did all that she could for the good of those who came to her, and most of all, for the small boys and girls, for whom she felt still more love than for the big ones, and those, whose father and mother were too poor to pay for them she taught for no pay but the joy it gave her to be with them, for they were all good, or if they were not so at first, were soon

GOODY TWO SHOES.

made so by the care she took of
them. We have told you that the
school where she taught was that
which had been kept by Mrs.
Williams. The room was large,
and, as she knew that boys and
girls are made with a wish to
move from place to place, she put
her blocks of wood, or *a, b, c*'s, all
round the school, so that each
one had to get up from his seat
and fetch a block or spell a word
when it came to his turn; which
both kept them in health, and put

the words in their minds more than if they could have made them with more ease. The school-house was in quite a bad state ; the walls were not firm, so that it was not quite safe, and the whole house was in great want of paint. When they told this to Sir William Dove, he had it built up new, and paid for it from his own purse, and till that could be done, Mr. Grove, who had a farm with a good house on it, was so kind as to let Miss Two Shoes

have his large hall to teach in.
The house built by Sir William,
had cut in the stone on the top of
the door, a boy on the ice with
skates on and a sled in his hand.
Miss Two Shoes wrote a verse to
suit it, and had it cut on the stone,
and paid for it from her own
purse. While Miss Two Shoes
was at Mr. Grove's, which was
in the midst of the town, she
taught all the boys and girls in
the day-time, but that was not
all ; Mr. Grove's maids, and all the

maids who did not live too far off, she taught to read and write when it was dark and the lamps were lit. Those whose homes were near hers, knew how good Miss Two Shoes was, (and in fact no young girls in all the town were as good as she was,) and they gave her one day a young lark. Now there were some boys and girls whose way it was to lie in bed far too late; she thought the lark might be of use to her and to those she taught, for it would tell them when to get up. " For he that is fond of his bed and lies till noon, lives but half of his days ; the rest are lost in sleep, which is a kind of death." When she had had the lark some days, a poor lamb lost its dam, and the man on whose farm it was meant to kill it, but she bought it of him, and brought it home with her, to play with the boys and girls, and to teach them when to go to bed, for it was a rule with the wise men of that age to

" Rise with the lark and lie down
with the lamb."

To this lamb she gave the name
of Will, and a pure white lamb
he was.   As soon as Tip the lark
and Will the baa lamb were
brought to the school, that wise
rogue Black Ralph made up this
verse, which all good boys and
girls should get by heart :

" Early to bed and early to rise,
Is the way to be healthy, wealthy,
and wise."

When some days had gone by, some one gave Miss Madge a gift of a small dog, who was at all times full of fun, and would jump and skip round the room, so they gave him the name of Jumper. The work that Jumper had to do, was to keep the door, for they soon found that he would let no one in or out, if Miss Madge did not say that they might go. Billy the baa lamb was full of fun, and all the boys and girls were fond of him: so Miss Two Shoes made it a rule, that they who were the best in school-hours, should take Will home at night, to take their bag of books on his back, and bring it to the school the next day. When school was at an end, Miss Two Shoes would play with the boys and girls at games in which there was no harm, or else she told them tales to help them to learn what was right, or to make them laugh. It came to pass, one day, as she did so, that a man came in with the sad news that the father of Sally Jones was thrown from his horse, and that there was no hope that he would get well; in fact, the man who brought the news said that he was all but dead when he left him. All the school was in tears, and the man who brought the news, had to go back, but when he went, Miss Two Shoes, though not one of the boys or girls knew it, told Tom the dove to go home with the man, and bring a note to tell her how Mr. Jones did. As soon as the man was gone, they saw that the dove was not to be found, and while they thought of him, their minds did not dwell so much on their grief for Mr. Jones and poor Sally, for they were all fond of Tom, and felt sad to lose him. She then told them a tale of Mr. Lovewell, the father of Miss Lucy, and how he lost all his wealth, and of all the bad luck he had. When the tale came to an end they heard a noise, like the flap of a bird's wing, at the blind.

"Bow, wow, wow!" said Jumper, and he tried to leap up and get out of the door ; the boys and girls could not think what made him do so ; but Miss Madge knew what it was. It did not take her long to raise up the sash, and, like Noah in the Ark, she drew in a dove ; it was Tom, with a note tied to his wing. As soon as she put him down on the floor, he went up to poor Sally ; Miss Madge took the note from him, and he cried, " Coo, coo, coo !" as

much as to say, " There, read it."
Now this dove had come five
times ten miles, in less than an
hour, and brought the good news
that there was no more fear that
Mr. Jones would die.

Miss Madge tried all the time
to do good, and thought she could
not do too much for those who
had done the least thing to serve
her.   These kind thoughts made
her try to do more and more for
Mr. Grove, and the rest of those
who had been so kind to her.

Most of their lands were fields where grass grew, and the best of all their crops was their hay ; but, for some years, a great part of their hay had been lost by rain. Now Miss Madge got a glass which would tell them when they could mow their grass, and have no fear that it would get wet ; they all came to her to ask her if it would rain soon, and by that means got in all their hay, and let none of it get wet ; while most of that on the farms near the next town, was lost by the rain. This made a great noise in the land, and the folks who had farms some way off, were in such a rage, that at first they did not know what to do. Then they said she was a witch, and sent old Gaffer Goosecap (a man who had more love for talk than for his own work) to find out some proof that she was so. This man, who had not much sense, came by chance to her school, and saw her, as she went up and down the room, with

Black Ralph on her left arm, the
dove on her right, the lark on her
head, and the lamb and the dog
by her side ; the man thought this
so strange that he cried out, " A
witch! a witch! a witch!" When
she saw him she gave a laugh
and said, " A man who can guess
all things ! a man who can guess
all things!" and then he went off.
But it did not end thus, for they
sent for Miss Madge and took her
to court, and there all her friends
went too, to see what could be

done for her. There was at court, a judge who had not seen much of the world, and knew still less of the law ; he did not know how to act, and though no one had said one word to prove that she was not a good girl, he thought he must ask her who she could bring to prove that she bore a good name. " Who can you bring to prove that I am a bad girl, sir ?" said she. " There are not a few folks who will come to help me, if need be, but I doubt if there is one man here who is so weak as to think that there is such a thing as a witch. If I am a witch, there is my charm ;" [and she gave them a glass such as we use to tell when it will rain, and when it will be fine ;] " it is with this," said she, " that I have taught those who live near me, when it will rain, and when it will not." All who were there gave a loud laugh, and Sir William Dove, who was on the bench, told those who found fault with her, that he did not know how they

could be such fools as to think
there was such a thing as a witch.
"It is true," said he, "that some
good folks, who had done no harm,
have been made to bear great pain,
and some of them have lost their
lives, just for this same thing that
made you bring this poor girl here.
It is a thing that must cause shame
to our church, to our laws, to our
land, and to our good sense, but I
will tell you a true tale. There
was once in this land far to the
west of this town, a good girl,

fond of work; but when she grew old and could not work much they said of her the same things which you have said of poor Madge now. When the hogs grew sick and died, or when the cows did not give much milk they all said it was this poor thing's fault. If a horse got to be lame they said he had her in his head; if it blew a gale, some one said they had seen Jane Giles ride on the stick of a broom through the air. These, and some more wild tales, which it would make you laugh to hear, ran in the heads of all the poor folks who had not the sense to know that such things could not be true. At the door of each house, you might have seen the shoe of a horse stuck up with a nail, with the heels up ; and they made use of all sorts of tricks to vex her. Such was their rage, and their wish to do her harm, that some of them went to beg Mr. Williams, the priest of that town, not to let her come to church ; and at last they said that she should not come. But he said that in this they should not have their way, and he gave poor old Jane a nook in one of the aisles for her own, where she might kneel and pray to God in the best way she could. This made the rage of the men of that town grow more and more, and they would not let her have her share of the sum that was laid by for the poor of the town who were too old to work; and they would have been glad to let her starve to death, if Mr. Williams, with his good, kind heart, had not come to her aid.   But I will go on to the end of my tale, in which you will find that the true cause of such a thing is, want of wealth, old age, or want of sense ; and that no one can pass for a witch if they are not poor and old, or if they do not live in a place where the folks have not a grain of good sense.   When some years had gone by, a brother of hers died in a great town, far from her home, who, though he would not part with a cent till his life was at an end, at his death had to leave her a great sum, for he could not take it with him, and he had no friends but Jane. This made a great change in Jane's life ; she was no more Jane, but Miss Giles ; she took off her old gown and put on one that was clean and new. Those who had done her the most harm, paid their court to her, and the Judge, who had been more harsh to her than

all the rest, came to wish her joy;
and though some hogs died, and
more than one horse went lame,
and the wind at times blew a
strong gale, yet no one now said
it was the fault of Miss Giles;
and hence it is plain, as I said
some time since, that one must be
poor and old and live in a place
where they have no sense, or she
can not pass for a witch. Mr.
Williams, who was fond of a joke
and could make one at all times
with great ease, said, more than

once, that if there was a time
when Jane ought to have the name
of a witch, it was when her brother left her all his wealth, for that
with the sum that he left her, she
did more kind acts to the poor
and the sick, than all the rich folks
for ten miles round. Then Sir
William said how sad it made
him to see that the poor folks had
no more sense than to think that
there was such a thing as a witch.
Then he spoke of Miss Madge;
he told them how good she was,

what good sense she had, and how well she spent her time. Sir Charles Jones by this time thought so much of Miss Madge, that he told her he would give her a large sum if she would come and teach his child, and keep house for him. This she did not think best to do, but in a few months, when Sir Charles Jones grew ill and sent for her, she went ; and she was so wise in her care of the house, and so kind to him and his child, that he would not let her go back, but

told her he would like to make
her his wife. It made her glad to
think that he was so kind to her,
and thought so well of her as to
wish her to be his wife, but she
said that she did not think it right
to be so, till he had first made his
will, and in it left a great sum for
his child. So to please her he did so.
When this was done, and the day
had come, all the folks came in
crowds to see her wed, for all
were fond of her. But just
as the priest took the book in

his hand, to read the words that would have made them one, a man in a rich dress ran through the church door, and cried out "Stop, stop, stop!" This gave a great fright to all the folks that were there, and most of all to the bride that was to be, and Sir Charles Jones. The rich man who had come in, spoke first to Sir Charles and Miss Madge, and said that he would like to say a few words to them. He spoke so low that none but those who stood close by could hear what he said; and the folks did not know what to think when they saw Sir Charles stand as still as death, and his bride cry and faint in his arms. But this, that they thought was grief, they saw change all at once to a flood of joy, for this young man, in his rich dress, was the same small boy whom you heard of some time since, when he took the end of his coat to wipe the tears from his sister's face, the day he left her to go to sea; in short, it was Tommy Two Shoes, the brother of Miss Madge, who was just come home from the sea, where he had made a great sum; and as he heard, as soon as he came to land, that his sister was to be made a wife that day, he rode post, to give her the wealth that he thought was fit for such a bride; and he told her he would give her a large sum, and then he should still have some to keep. She and Sir Charles Jones were wed in tears, but they were tears of joy.

When Sir Jones had made her his wife, she had a house built in the town for a school house, and put a poor man and his wife there, who knew well how to read and write and do sums, and she thought that the poor would see how good they were, and would try to be like them; here she had all the poor boys and girls taught to read and write, and she told the good dame who taught the school, more than all, to teach the girls how to sew, and the man, who had been a smith by trade, taught some of the lads his art, so that they could make some things that were of use, some of which they gave each year to Madge to show her how well they could work. They most of them grew to be good men, and had great cause to thank God who gave them such a friend as Goody Two Shoes; by her care they had been taught to fear God, to love those whose homes were near theirs, and to be kind and not wish to hurt those who had done them wrong. They were taught, too, to speak the truth at all times and not to waste their time. she let the man and his wife use the school house, and yet pay no rent for it; and that was not all; she gave them a large sum at the end of each year to buy their food and clothes ; and she gave to the boys and girls of the school all the books they had need of. Madge Jones did not cease to think of her good friend Mr. Smith ; she sent him from where he was, to a church where they could pay him well, and to which she had the right to send whom she thought best, and she gave him, too, a large sum to buy beds and chairs and so forth for his new home, and to paint it from the roof to the ground. Sir Thomas Gripe, the same man who had been so harsh with Madge's father, was so to Mr. Smith too. Madge went to law with him and took Mr. Smith's part; the cause was tried, and it was not hard to prove that Mr. Smith was in the right. Then, as it was made clear that Sir Thomas had done some things that it was a shame for a judge to do, they would no more let him be one. This was a sharp stroke to a man like him, and there came one still worse, for a niece of his who had a right to the farm of Mouldwell, laid claim to it, and got it, and by and by when she had a mind to sell it, she gave Madge the first chance to buy it. She bought the whole and made of it small farms, that the poor might no more have a rich and hard man to deal with. This was a great grief to Sir Thomas, who, from this time, had no more good luck, and he soon got rid of all his wealth. But Madge said that all ought to be kind to his boys and girls; " for they," said she, " are by no means to blame for the bad acts of their father." She took great care of the poor ; and to cause them to go to church, she said she would give a loaf at church to all

who would like one. This brought
some to church who, if it had not
been for that, would not have come,
and by and by they thought more
of the things it was right for them
to do, and then they came for what
was worth more to them than
bread. When two young folks of
the town were wed, she gave them
a bed and some chairs for their
new home. As long as God gave
her life, she was kind to the small
boys and girls of the town, she let
them come to her house, on the

first day of the week, and taught
them what good boys and girls
ought to know. Then she gave
them some good food, and gave
them such books as she thought
would best teach them to be good,
and at her death, she left them each
a small sum in her will. There was
one thing in her will that we must
not fail to speak of ; it is that she
left some land, that they were to
plant each year with beans for all
the poor who would come to get
them, for the use of their wives and

boys and girls, but if a man took them to sell, he was to have no more. And the work on these lots was to be paid for by the rent of a farm which she left just for that. In short, the child of a poor man was to her as if it had been her own ; she did all she could to heal the sick, and she was a kind friend to all who were in need. All who knew her felt that they ought to bless God for her life, and her death was a great grief to all who were in the land.

TOM THUMB.

In the days of good King Arthur, Merlin, a wise man for the times in which he was born, left his home for a short trip, and once, as the day was hot, and he felt as if he would like to rest, he thought he would stop and ask for some food. Just as he thought thus he came to the house of a good man, who did not mind work, and who was glad to get all his gains in a right way. The wife of this man, who was glad to be of use to one

who came to her hot and in need
of rest, lost no time, but brought
him some milk in a bowl made of
wood, and some brown bread on
a plate that was made of wood
too. Merlin could not fail to see,
that all the things in the house
were so neat and clean that
no fault could be found with
them, but though there was a
place for all things, and each in
its own place, yet all the while he
was there, he did not see a smile
on the man's face, nor on that of

his wife. So he made up his
mind to ask them the cause of
their grief, and they told him that
they both felt sad all the time, for
they had no child. The poor wife
said, with tears in her eyes, that
she thought no one in the world
would be so gay as she, if she had
a son, though he were but as big
as the thumb of his father. Merlin gave a laugh, when he thought
of a boy the size of a man's thumb,
and as soon as he got home, he
sent for the Queen of the fairies,

(whom he knew quite well) and told her the wish of the good man and his wife to have a son, though he should not grow more than to the size of his father's thumb. The Queen of the fairies thought it was a fine plan, and said she would grant their wish at once. So the good man's wife had a son, who in half an hour grew as tall as his father's thumb. The Queen of the fairies came in through a small hole in the wall as the mother sat up in bed to look at her child. The Queen gave the child a kiss and said the name of it should be Tom Thumb, then she gave a call to some more fairies, to come from Fairy Land to clothe her new pet :

An oak leaf hat he had for his crown,
His shirt it was by silk worms spun ;
His coat was made of thistle down,
And both his pants with points were done,
His socks, of the rind of a pear, they tie
With a lash which they took from his ma's
    bright eye
His shoes were made of a mouse's skin,
With soft fur out and soft fur in.

Tom grew till he was the size of
his father's thumb, which was not
a large thumb, and then grew no
more; but as years went by, he
grew quite sly and full of tricks,
which his mother did not whip
him for, as she ought to have done,
so that when he could play with
the boys for beans, and had lost
all his own, his way was to creep
in the boys' bags, hide all he could
in his clothes, and then come out
to play.   But one day, as he got
out of a bag · of beans, the boy

whose bag it was, by chance saw
him. " Ah ha, my young Tom
Thumb!" said the boy, " have I
caught you at your bad tricks at
last! Now I will show you how bad
it is to be a thief.   Then he drew
the strings tight around his neck,
and shook the bag hard ; the
beans hurt Tom's arms and legs
and thighs a great deal, which
made him beg to be let out, and
he said he would do no more such
things.

One day, it was but a few days

from the time that he was in the
bean bag, his mother made a batter pudding, and that he might
watch her mix it, he got up on the
edge of the bowl, but his foot by
chance gave a slip and he fell up
to his neck in the batter, and as
his mother did not see him, she
gave the pudding a stir which hid
him quite, and put him in the pot
to boil. It soon grew so hot that
it made Tom kick and plunge;
and when his mother saw the
pudding jump up and down in

such a strange way, she thought there was a witch in it; and as a man came by just at that time, she in great haste gave him the pudding; he put it in his bag, and off he went. As soon as Tom could get the batter out of his mouth, he gave a loud cry, which put the poor man in such a fright that he flung the pudding down on the ground, and ran off as fast as he could run. The pudding broke in small bits by the fall, Tom was set free and went home to his

TOM THUMB.

mother, who gave him a kiss and
put him to bed. Tom Thumb's
mother once took him with her,
when she went to milk the cow,
and as it blew hard that day, she
tied him with a piece of thread to
the stalk of a plant, that he might
not be blown out of her reach.
The cow thought his oak leaf hat
was good for food, so she took
him, and the plant he was tied to,
up in her mouth, all at once.
When the cow shut her teeth to
chew the plant, Tom, in a fright at

her great teeth, which he thought
would crush him to bits, cried out,
" Mother, mother ?" as loud as he
could bawl. " Where are you,
Tom, my dear Tom?" said his
mother. " Here, mother, here, in
the red cow's mouth." When his
mother heard this, she gave a cry,
and wrung her hands, but the cow,
who did not know what to make
of such an odd noise in her throat,
could not keep her mouth shut,
and so she let him drop out.
His mother put him in her lap

and ran home with him. Tom's father made him a whip out of a rye straw, to drive the cows with, and one day when he was in the field he fell in a small ditch. A crow, who flew by, took him up with a grain of corn, and flew with him to a strong fort, where a great man ten feet high had his home. It was close to the sea. There the crow left him, and old Grumbo, the tall man, who soon came to walk on the top of his fort, took Tom in his mouth like a pill, clothes and all. But Tom ran round in his mouth, which did not feel good to him, so he took him out of his mouth and threw him in the sea. Then, the first thing he knew, he was down the throat of a great fish. This fish was soon caught and sent as a gift to King Arthur. When they went to eat it, at the first stroke of the knife out came Tom Thumb, to the great joy of all who were there. The King made him his dwarf; he was the pet of the whole court,

and by his gay pranks, he made
the Queen and knights of the
court laugh a great deal. The
King, when he rode on a horse,
would now and then take Tom in
his hand, and if a storm of rain
came on, he hid in the King's vest,
and there he slept till the rain was
all gone. The King would now
and then ask Tom who his father
and mother were ; when Tom told
him that they were poor folks, the
King led him to the place where
he kept his gold and so forth, and

told him he should go to see his
friends and take with him as much
gold as he could lift.   Tom got a
small purse, and put in it a piece
of gold worth just six cents : he
found it quite hard to get such a
weight on his back, and when he
had been two days and two nights
on the road, he got safe to the
house of his father.   His mother
met him at the door, half dead
with his long walk, for in two
days and two nights he had gone
quite half a mile with a huge piece

of gold as big as the head of a pin
on his back. His father and mother were glad to see him, and still
more glad when they found he had
brought such a large bag of gold
with him. They put him in the
shell of a nut, by the side of the
fire, and fed him for three days on
a beech nut, which made him sick,
for a whole nut ought to last him
a month. Tom got well, but
could not walk back to court,
for there had been a hard rain ; so
his mother took him in her hand

and with one puff blew him to King Arthur's court; at that time they had balls and tilts and all such things at the court. Tom said and did all he could to make the Queen and knights laugh, and was so full of fun, and ran round so much, that it made him ill, and they thought he could not get well. Just then the Queen of the fairies came in a car, drawn by mice who knew how to fly; she took Tom by her side, drove through the air, and did not stop till she got to her own home. There she soon made Tom well, and then let him see all the gay sports of Fairy Land. When she thought it was time for him to go back, she told the wind to blow, and put Tom where he could feel the full force of it. It blew him straight to the court of King Arthur. But just as Tom, still high in the air, came in the yard of the King's house, the cook, by chance, came that way, with the King's great bowl of oat meal,

(King Arthur was fond of oat
meal,) and poor Tom Thumb fell
right in the midst of it, and the
great splash he made, threw the
hot oat meal in the cook's eyes.
Down went the bowl. " Oh,
dear, oh dear!" cried Tom. " Oh,
oh, oh!" said the cook, with a
great roar, and the nice oat meal
ran down the great drain. The
cook was a great, cross man with
a red face, and he swore to the
King, that Tom meant to do it;
so they took him and tried him,

and said he should have his head
cut off. When Tom heard this,
it did not please him at all, for he
thought it hard that he should lose
his life for so small a crime. By
chance there stood there a man
who kept a mill, and who had not
the good sense to keep his mouth
shut, so Tom gave a good spring,
and in a trice found that he was
down the man's throat ; but no one
had seen him jump, and the man
down whose throat he had sprung,
knew no more than the rest that

he was there.   As Tom was lost,
and they could not cut off the
head of a man whom they could
not find, the court broke up, and
off went the man who had Tom
in his mouth, to his mill.   But
Tom did not leave him long at
rest; he gave a roll on this side
and a roll on that, and fell here
and there, till the man thought a
witch must have tried to play
some prank with him, and he sent
for a leech to cure him.   When
the leech came, Tom took it in his

head to dance and sing, which put
the leech in just as great a fright as
the man of the mill, so he sent in
great haste for five more men of his
own trade, and five times five wise
men, to see if they knew what was
to be done in so strange a case.
While all these men set their heads
to work to think, and set their
tongues to work to talk, the man
who had the mill, (for it took
them a long time to make up their
minds what to say, by chance gave
a great yawn, and Tom, who was

quite glad of a chance to get out,
gave a jump, and down he came
on his feet, on the floor, in the
midst of them all.   The wise men
all gave a laugh, but the man of
the mill (who by the by was not a
wise man) did not laugh.   It did
not please him to think that
so small a thing as Tom Thumb
had made him make such a fuss,
so he flew in a great rage, caught
hold of poor Tom, and threw him
in the deep stream on which the
mill stood.   A fine large trout

swam by just then, and took him
up in his mouth in less time than
it takes a dog to wag his tail.
The trout was soon caught, and
sold for a great sum to a man who
had come to the town to buy some
fish for his Lord to eat. The
Lord thought it was too fine a
fish for him to keep, so he gave
it to the King, who was quite
fond of fine trout. The King
gave it his cook and told him to
cook it at once. When the cook
cut the trout in two bits, to broil

it, he found poor Tom, and ran
with him straight to the King.
But the King had some things of
great weight to talk of with his
knights, so he told the cook not to
bring Tom Thumb to him that
day, but to wait some days.   The
cook made up his mind that he
would keep him safe this time;
and as he had some fear that he
would get off, as he had done the
last time he took him to the King,
he put him in a mouse-trap, and
left him there to play as best he

could, and peep through the wires. Tom had to stay there a whole week ; then the King sent for him. He told him not to fear that he would kill him for what he had done to the oat meal, for he would think of it no more. He told them to make him a new suit of clothes, and he made him a knight.

His shirt was made of a white moth's wings,
His boots were made of grey doves' skins,
His pants were made of a young rat's hide,
A pin for a sword hung by his side,
A mouse for a horse he used to ride.

With this fine dress, and on
this fine horse, he went to hunt
with the King and his knights,
who all gave a loud laugh when
they saw Tom and his fine steed,
who knew how to prance as well
as their steeds did.   As they rode
by a farm-house one day, a cat
gave a spring from a hole in the
wall near the door ; she took up
in her mouth and claws the mouse
and poor Tom, and lost no time,
but set to work to eat the mouse,
but Tom, bold as could be, drew

his sword and stuck it in the cat, who was then quite glad to let him fall. The king and his lords and knights saw that Tom would fall if some of them did not help him, and if he fell, he might break his leg, or his arm, or his back, and, as they were all fond of him, this would have made them quite sad, so they all went to his aid, and one of the lords caught him in his hat. But poor Tom had a long scratch on his face, and three or four on his hands, and some more too, though his clothes had done a good deal to save him. But they, too, were much torn by the claws of the cat. In this sad state they took him home, where a bed of down was made for him, just as big a one as you would need for a small doll less than an eighth of a yard long. The frame and posts of the bed were made from the tooth of some great beast ; some men who knew how to carve such things, had cut it with great care ; it was as white as snow. The

Queen of the fairies came and took him back to Fairy Land, where she kept him for some years; then she gave him a dress of bright green, and, with a puff of her breath, sent him once more through the air to the earth. King Arthur was dead at that time; and Thunstone was King in his stead. The folks came far and near to look at him; and the King to whose court they took him, told him that he should be glad to know who he was, whence he came, and in what place he made his home.　Tom said

> My name is Tom Thumb ;
> From the Fairies I come ;
> When King Arthur shone,
> This court was my home.

I made him laugh with all his might,
And by him I was made a knight.
I think these folks must be deaf and dumb
If they have not heard of Sir Thomas Thumb.

The King was quite struck with this speech; in fact, he thought so much of it, that he told them to make a small chair, that Tom might sit close by his throne, and

he made them build, too, a house
of gold, a span high, for Tom
Thumb to live in. He gave him,
too, a coach drawn by six small
mice. This did not please the
Queen, for the King did not give
her a new coach, when he gave
Tom one ; so she made up her
mind that she would put an end
to Tom's joy, and went to the
King and told him that Tom had
been rude to her. This was not
true, for Tom was rude to no one ;
but the Queen made the King

think it was true, and he sent for
Tom in a rage. Tom, to get out of
the way of his wrath, crept in a snail
shell that had no snail in it, for
the snail had long been dead.
There he lay until he thought he
should starve for the want of food.
when, as he gave a peep out of the
shell he saw a fine, large moth
which had flown down and stood
on the ground close to him.　He
now thought he might dare to come
out, so he got up on the moth's
back, and the moth took wing

and flew up in the air with Tom on his back. Off he flew, from field to field, from tree to tree, till at last he flew back to the King's court. The King and Queen, the lords, the knights, all strove to catch the moth, but could not. At length poor Tom, who had no rein to guide his steed, and did not know what to hold on to, could not keep his seat, but as the moth gave a quick start in a way he did not think it would go, he fell. He fell in a white jar which the late rain had made quite full, and then he thought he should drown, but just in time they took him out. The Queen said that she would not rest in peace till he had his head cut off; and while they went to get the axe to cut his head off, they put him in a mouse-trap to keep him safe. But the cat came in, and when she saw what was in the trap move, she thought it must be a mouse; so she gave the trap two or three pats with her paw, which broke it, and then Tom was free. But sad to say, in a few hours from that time, a spider, who took him for a fly, made at him. Tom drew his sword and fought like a brave man, but the breath of the spider made him faint; he fell and was slain:

He fell dead on the ground where late he had
    stood,
And the spider drank up the last drop of his
    blood.

King Thunstone put on black, and so did his whole court, for Tom Thumb. They made him a grave at the foot of a bush where the first rose of Spring came out each year; and they put a pure, white stone at the head of his grave, on which you might read these lines.

Here lies Tom Thumb, King Arthur's knight,
Whose death was from a spider's bite.
He was well known in Arthur's court;
His jokes were good and made great sport;
And when he to the hunt did go
'Twas to a mouse that he cried whoa!
His days in joy and mirth were spent,
His death to grief and woe gave vent.
Wipe, wipe your eyes and shake your head
And cry, Our dear Tom Thumb is dead!